Magic Stones

McQueen

Magic Stones

Paperback Edition First Publishing in Great Britain
in 2014 by aSys Publishing

eBook Edition First Publishing in Great Britain
in 2014 by aSys Publishing

ISBN: 978-0-9929796-6-9

aSys Publishing
http://www.asys-publishing.co.uk

Disclaimer

Contents

Chapter 1

The Holding Station

"What the hell... what's happening?" With the veil of oblivion gradually lifting, Andy began to realise he had landed in a more bizarre place than he had ever imagined. New experiences generally excited him - never more so than on a night out with his friends, Dave and Joe - but this was really weird. Most surprising was the absence of a woman lying next to him. This was curious given his usual success rate. It was the "other worldliness" that made him wary; the absence of familiar smells and the peculiar silence, only interrupted by the roaring in his ears. With fear enveloping him like a wave crashing over his body, he was desperate for a distraction and turned his thoughts to the previous evening.

As usual, the night had started well with the three friends meeting in their bar, Dreamlands. It was a mediocre place, hurriedly and cheaply constructed in the 1980s for teens and twenties eager to spend their wages on alcohol fuelled fun and frivolity. With punters now opting for trendier venues, Dreamlands was sliding downhill to nowhere. The interior had become dull and dreary with old, threadbare, carpets, sticky from spilled drinks. Shoes stuck to the grubby nylon pile and mellow lighting, which once created a romantic ambience, now revealed its sordid decline.

The friends were not at all concerned with their surroundings; of greater importance to them were the fine beers on offer and their jovial landlord. It was almost a religious rite with the three of them to stay at Dreamlands right up to closing time, when they set about choosing their next port of call; there was a multitude of clubs and bars available to them. Moving on would mean the trio would be separated, and Dave and Joe would be lost to Andy for another week, never a pleasant prospect for him to entertain, and he'd never been good at dealing with disappointment.

Towards the end of the evening he'd struck up a conversation with a woman he'd met a few weeks earlier. Not, he thought, a substitute for his friends, or the most entertaining company, although acceptable in the circumstances. But... where had she gone? Why wasn't she here? Feeling restless and more than a little crestfallen, Andy decided to catch up with his friends, convinced that he would feel better when he was with them again. He tried to stand but found, to his horror, that he was paralysed. Being unable to move was terrifying and the absence of anything familiar disorientated him, making matters even worse. Covered in a shroud of the finest mist, he lay motionless and frightened, trying to think of plausible explanations; the worst hangover of all, time? A hospital admission? Also confusing was the absence of worldly references; there was no background noise, no traffic, no children, and no smells of any kind. Eventually, and grudgingly, Andy conceded that his reasoning was well wide of the mark and not at all realistic. The fact of the matter was that he was dead and nothing he could do was going to change that. Fear and self-pity engulfed him. Dead at twenty-four! "It's so unfair," he whimpered, and wept for his own misfortune, grateful that nobody was there to witness his weakness. For a moment he thought he glimpsed a man walking in the distance, a rather stooped old man, wearing a long, grey, robe, whose face and head were covered in scraggy white hair. Andy decided against attracting his attention (if he was really there) as he seemed too old to be of any help to anyone.

Still frightened, Andy wasn't comforted by the clouds and mist preventing him from having a clear view of his surroundings. To compose himself, he resorted to a trick he learned as a child, and made himself think about something else, Dave and Joe.

Their friendship was an unusual mix as Andy's lifestyle contrasted starkly with that of his friends. Trading in heroin met all of Andy's financial needs and enabled him to live the uncluttered life that suited him. He could avoid the boring and unpleasant work which burdened his friends. The daily grind was not for him, but he acknowledged that his friends enjoyed the fruits of their labours; decent cars and clothes and an amusing life-style. Andy thought, however, that the price they paid was too great. Now, of course, they were lost to him forever. Silently, out of nowhere, the stooping, elderly, man appeared.

"Good morning, I'm Gabriel."

"Good morning, I'm Andy."

What he really wanted to say was "How can you tell what time it is? The light doesn't seem to vary."

"Come with me," the old man said.

"Impossible, I'm afraid, I can't move, "Andy replied.

"Perhaps with a little effort...." Gabriel smiled encouragingly.

Cautiously, Andy unfolded his six foot frame, taking a little longer than usual as there was still some stiffness in his joints and muscles, although the pains in his hands and feet had gone. Oddly for a man not known for concern about his appearance, he tried to make himself more presentable.

"Have you realised where you are?" enquired Gabriel.

"I think I'm dead, "Andy said nervously, "but not sure where I am."

Gabriel guided Andy through the vast, empty, space, talking fondly of the place which he called the Holding Station.

"You were lucky to get a place here, my boy. It was touch and go for a while. Your admission was a contentious issue. The Influencing Team couldn't agree about you, and Barrie had to use her casting vote, which is all but unheard of. We're off to see her now," added Gabriel.

Andy found Gabriel's presence reassuring. It helped to quell his anxiety which had increased when he saw a modest building looming through the thinning clouds. As they approached the building, the aroma of fresh coffee grew stronger and Andy was surprised that his desire for something so homely was so strong. Gabriel led Andy into a building which reminded him of the scores of Social Security offices he'd known and disliked. They always had a notice inviting comment about the quality and nature of the services provided. Andy had frequently amused himself by drafting replies: "I offer my heartfelt thanks for the index-linked increase in my benefit"; "I really would prefer the attractive blond to process my next claim." On other occasions, especially when his request had been turned down, his thoughts could be much darker.

The grim exterior and entrance gave way to greater comfort inside. Quality carpet cushioned every sound. The reception area boasted several luxurious couches and chairs placed tastefully around the large room. The gentle colour scheme promoted a sense of tranquility. Several colourful paintings completed the decor, the seven doors, each a colour of the rainbow, led from the room. Gabriel made for the green door, the middle one on the right hand side of the room. The sign on the door said "Barrie". Gabriel's knock activated the mechanical door. He entered, closely followed by Andy, who found himself in a well-appointed, comfortable, room. Andy didn't feel comfortable in himself, however. The blinds on the windows were closed and the feeling that he had no choice about being there made him feel isolated and vulnerable, and this caused him to be angry and hostile.

"Thank you, Gabriel, you can leave us now. Welcome, Andy, would you like coffee? It might be comforting to have something familiar amidst so much that's strange and new."

"Er, yes, that would be great," Andy said, with feeling.

"Black or white?"

"White, two sugars, please."

"We've had so many young people who seem unable to last more than an hour or two without coffee, that we eventually thought it would make sense to have a Starbucks of our own."

Barrie moved away from the coffee machine, her rotund figure moved effortlessly away from the coffee machine whilst indicating with her cup that Andy choose one of the elegant lounge chairs. Andy, unhappy with his predicament, and impatient to learn what lay in store for him made no effort to hide his annoyance as he sat down.

"I've been told you're now aware of your death. Perhaps you're less knowledgeable about what goes on here, so I hope to fill in some of the gaps for you this morning."

"Now she's at it," thought Andy," how on earth does she know it's morning?"

Meanwhile, Barrie went on to confirm that Andy's admission to the Holding Station had been anything but straight forward. The Influencing Team had been evenly split on the issue and she had used her casting vote to support his acceptance. Barrie explained that she'd based her decision on Andy's earthly history.

"Thanks for that, Barrie, any chance of another coffee?"

Fixing him with a glacial stare over her horn-rimmed glasses, Barrie said "Help yourself."

The little confidence that had returned to Andy ebbed away; his emotions were in such a tangle that he was quite exhausted.

Barrie was still talking. "I've assigned you to the Earthly Team. I feel you'll benefit from a broader, deeper, knowledge of the human race. Spending time with, and working alongside your colleagues should help you to achieve this. Do you have any questions?" Barrie prompted.

"No," Andy replied hastily.

His earlier indiscretion had left him more than slightly apprehensive, and his desire to retreat was overwhelming. He needed to be alone, to take stock of his new "life". Barrie pushed the green button on her desk and, almost immediately, a knock heralded the opening of the automatic doors, revealing a small man with tiny eyes and a sallow complexion who was almost bald.

"This is Jeff. He'll show you round the Earthly Team's accommodation and explain the systems to you. Don't attempt too much on your first day; we don't want to inundate you when you've only just arrived. I'll contact you when necessary but, for now, goodbye," said Barrie. Later, Gabriel joined Barrie. They both had reservations about Andy's ability to fit in and get along with the team, but neither voiced them. Instead, they relaxed with a gin and tonic, enjoying each other's company, and leaving contentious issues firmly to one side.

Chapter 2

"Isn't she a bitch," said Jeff.

Andy froze. It wasn't simply what Jeff had said, but that he said it a couple of feet away from Barrie's door. In fact, Jeff's indiscretion would come to nothing, but Andy wasn't to know that. He didn't know how his new world worked or how he would function within it, which was very unsettling.

Progress was slow as the pair navigated their way through the blankets of clouds, Jeff helping Andy to pick his way across this strange, new, landscape. Feeling stronger, and free of Gabriel and Barrie, Andy was eager to see more of his new home but, annoyingly, the fluffy white and grey clouds stacked up on top of each other, denying him a clear view. He felt trapped, isolated and uneasy in this strange, outlandish, place.

In time they reached their destination. The building was reminiscent of an aircraft hangar. It was wide, long, toweringly high, and constructed from corrugated iron and concrete. It exuded a cold, unwelcoming, atmosphere. Like Barrie's building, this one had the private rooms arranged around the sides of its imposing frame, but here there were partitions between the rooms and the main operating space. The name of each occupant was painted on the door. It seemed to Andy that the amateurish attempt to paint out the name of his predecessor suggested a hasty change of tenant.

"Having had five preparation days, you'll find everything you need has been provided. Rumour has it that your admission to the Holding Station was touch and go. Never known anybody to take so long to be assigned," said Jeff. He spent a little longer with Andy, helping him to familiarise himself with his room, before leaving with the promise to return later.

Glancing round his room, Andy was stunned to see it contained replicas of his earthly possessions. It was obvious they were replicas because there were no signs of damage or wear. Gone were the cigarette burns on the sofa, testaments to rowdy nights watching rugby matches on TV whilst drinking and consuming cocktails of illegal substances. The scratches on the table, caused by preparing food and drugs had disappeared, and the broken chair leg had been repaired at last. Flabbergasted, he sat on his bed and enjoyed the much improved mattress while trying to come to terms with the notion of eternity. Jeff barged back into his room without knocking and startled Andy back into reality. "How are we getting along, old chap? I said you'd find all you need. Come on, I'll introduce you to the rest of the gang and explain how we operate, I'll even give you the low down on them, but only if you promise not to tell." Andy didn't let on that he hadn't moved a muscle while Jeff had been gone, and that he'd sat on his bed rigid with fright. Jeff was irritatingly sociable whilst Andy was quite the opposite, feeling tired, bewildered, and in desperate need of solitude. He briefly considered negotiating some more free time but, in the end, decided against it. He didn't want to upset Jeff or damage his own position at such an early stage. Having no influence to exert, he was forced to accept Jeff's suggestion and accompany him to the main part of the building.

At one end of the vast space he could make out half a dozen desks and chairs, two of which appeared to be unused. The old, wooden, desks were relics of the 1950s and were almost lost in the enormous room. Each desk bore the damage accumulated over the years, like the names of sweethearts carved behind the teacher's back. The desks were positioned some distance apart and each had a monitor and a telephone. On two of the desks there were such mounds of paperwork that it was difficult to find the 'phones when they rang. On one unoccupied desk stood a long-forgotten cup of coffee. Its dried up dregs too stubborn to be washed away, it was destined for the bin.

To one side, and immediately behind where Andy was standing, was what could be loosely described as the lounge-dining area. There were several dining chairs placed around a circular, glass table. Beyond them were several lounge chairs and settees, peppered with cushions.

On the wall opposite the partition was a cheap sink sitting in a double draining board. On one side stood a coffee machine and the other was piled high with dirty dishes. Inevitably there would be some disgruntled comments made before Sarah relented and eventually washed them all. She and Peter were relaxing in the lounge when Jeff obliged them to end their conversation by insisting on introducing them to Andy. "Hello, I'm delighted to have somebody new here. It's been far too long since we had some new blood, if you know what I mean," said Sarah. "Sarah has the hots for me," Jeff whispered.

"For heaven's sake," thought Andy, "they're far too old to be interested in sex; they must be fifty, if not older."

Sarah continued with her friendly banter but Andy paid scant attention to what she said. He was thinking that if the rest of the team were as old as Peter and Sarah his sexual prowess would definitely not be needed. He wondered whether masturbation could ever compensate for the absence of a beautiful woman, preferably with long legs and a tight bum.

"Here's your desk. There are a few papers in the drawer; they were left by your predecessor. Take a look. Keep what you think might be useful and throw the rest away," said Jeff.

"What happened to him or her?" Andy asked.

"Shouldn't concern yourself with that lad." Said Jeff

Finding conversation a strain, and his surroundings confusing, Andy thought his plight was horrendous. He thought he would implode if he had to live in such a pitiful place with its equally pitiful inhabitants. All his concerns were swept aside by a sudden explosion that seemed to come from an invisible source at the far end of the room. Ignoring Andy's obvious distress, Jeff joked that the clock above the sink never kept the correct time. After a while, however, he showed Andy the cause of the thunder that was still rumbling. It came from deep inside a hole containing a mass of red, molten, rock, constantly swirling around, but unable to escape. Jeff explained that the movement resulted in eruptions that activated the fax machine that delivered the **requests** that the team handled.

"It's a relic from the past, like the furniture," said Jeff.

"And the people," thought Andy.

"When we receive a *request* the team discusses who is the most suitable to deal with it. If there's a disagreement, Barrie arbitrates."

"Ummm."

"Here's Sarah. I'll leave you to settle in and familiarise yourself with the contents of the desk. Don't want to get trapped, you see," said Jeff, hurrying away.

"I've just had a *request* for snow," said Sarah. "I remember years back a young girl made so many requests for snow that I became very fond of her. Her requests were more real than most; they were born out of despair, unlike most of the ones we get now. I blame the "wish-list" culture and the all pervading belief that Life has to be perfect and desires fulfilled at whatever cost. That philosophy alone has generated a huge amount of unnecessary work for the team."

Deeply averse to the bland instruction to "familiarise" himself with the contents of the desk, Andy was a little surly. Sarah detected this and retreated, allowing him to slip, unnoticed behind the partition to find sanctuary in his room.

Chapter 3

Lying on his bed, eyes tightly shut in an attempt to keep his new existence at bay, Andy was astounded by the sudden surge of loneliness that engulfed him. For the first time in years he longed for the company and comfort of his beloved mother, Vanessa. His need for parental comfort didn't extend to Stuart, his father, who was associated with anxiety and unhappiness.

The only child of Frederick and Jean, Vanessa was born and raised in a small village on the outskirts of Leeds, where she enjoyed a comparatively sheltered and comfortable life-style. Both her parents were teachers and there had been an inevitability about her following suit. Vanessa's academic achievements were respectable in all subjects apart from Art, in which she excelled. On the completion of her schooling, she was awarded a place at a prestigious university, and moved to London. Although the university had a reputation for producing some of the country's finest artists Vanessa, as a precautionary measure, trained as a teacher. She loved her life in London. She found its vibrancy intoxicating, grabbing all it had to offer with both hands. She was blissfully happy in her small, self-contained flat on the first floor of a large, Victorian, house. It was well situated and close to a tube station, so the rent was comparatively high, and Vanessa supplemented her income by working in a restaurant for a couple of nights and days each week.

She was delighted with her newly acquired independence, enriched by her many new friends and acquaintances. Throughout her childhood, Vanessa had enjoyed holidays with her parents when they had camped overseas. She had often forged brief, but intense, friendships against the backdrop of unfamiliar languages and cultures. She had continued her travels with carefully planned trips during long university vacations. She'd experienced a few romantic interludes, but nothing serious or lasting; she was far more serious about holding on to her freedom. On the completion of her studies, Vanessa chose to remain in London. It was a source of sadness for her parents, Frederick and Jean, that they saw little of their daughter once she had established her independence. They never uttered a word of reproach, their daughter's obvious happiness being some consolation to them. Her telephone calls were peppered with exciting descriptions of her life in London. On the night she called to tell them about her invitation to Gerry and Simon's dinner party, she was particularly exuberant. "Do you remember me telling you about Gerry, short for Geraldine, who's married to Simon, a city banker? You do, well Gerry has just completed a project with my class and is leaving the school. She's terribly interesting, drives a BMW sports car. Guess what, she's asked me to join her and her husband, along with a couple of friends, for dinner later this week. I'm the only one from the *whole* school who's been invited. Isn't that amazing? I'll ring and let you know how it all goes. Love to mum, bye."

As promised, Vanessa telephoned her dad a couple of nights after the dinner party, her voice brimming with excitement. Dispensing with formal pleasantries, she launched into her account of the dinner party, hardly missing a detail. "Simon's friend, Stuart, was there. He was particularly vexed to be invited as a last minute replacement for someone who'd cancelled. Apparently, he accepted the invitation in preference to a micro-waved dinner and a night on his own. For most of the evening he was engrossed in conversation with a colleague, so I was flabbergasted when he approached me at the end of the evening, and offered me a lift home. Then, guess what, he asked me out, said he'd pick me up at eight tomorrow. Gosh! What will I wear? Where will he take me? I'll, have to ask the others to move their bikes so they don't block the hallway. I don't want him falling over them, and I want to make a good impression on my first date. Hope you and mum are OK. Bye."

As a successful banker, Stuart enjoyed all the trappings of success. At the dinner party he'd sat several seats away from Vanessa; close enough to watch her without being too obvious. By the end of the evening, Stuart had decided to draw Vanessa away from the cluster for a private word. She was immediately captivated by his sophistication and wit. From then on he embarked on a campaign to entice her into his world where extravagance was the norm and fine dining and elite holidays came naturally, often at the expense of clients grateful for Stuart's clever handling of their investments.

"She will do nicely," said Stuart.

"Who?" asked Simon.

At their private club the food had been splendid. The club was their haven; the proprietor and his staff could always be relied upon to be discreet - a valuable asset on many occasions. Simon was astounded to learn that the relationship between Stuart and Vanessa had blossomed since their first dinner date; "a dear girl, but not Stuart's type." She was a beauty, that was for sure, but she was predictable and undemanding, quite the opposite of the glitzy, glamorous, models he usually preferred. But Stuart was not looking for a woman to "grace his arm". He wanted a wife to grace his night- time hours when he hadn't coaxed a woman into a bed elsewhere. The plan thrilled and delighted Simon, and explained why Vanessa had remained out of sight. Not since he'd first met her, after one of his wife's voyages into the world of the lower classes, had Vanessa received a mention. Stuart confided that Vanessa had "enough intelligence to parent a child" whilst he would be able to ensure it was "raised in my image." The clincher was that Vanessa knew nothing about his private world, leaving him free to pursue his sexual pleasures. Enjoying their evening in their usual fashion, the friends were oblivious to the fact that Gerry had deliberately withheld Stuart's invitation to her dinner party in an endeavour to weaken the bond between them.

Chapter 4

It was just six months after they met that Stuart proposed to Vanessa, shortly before whisking her off to Los Vegas where the couple were married. Vanessa was disappointed by Stuart's insistence that it would be a more romantic interlude if they married in private, "just the two of us". Imparting the plan to her parents was extremely difficult for Vanessa, who agreed with Stuart that she should meet them in her hometown. Stuart convinced Vanessa to meet Frederick and Jean in a restaurant rather than the family home; he was anxious to avoid recalling strong family memories which could sabotage his plans. Seated around the crisply laundered tablecloth, the expensive silverware wrapped in a large napkin, Vanessa began by apologising for Stuart's absence. "But, of course, he did telephone to ask for your consent, didn't he dad?" Frederick and Jean had little option but to give their blessing; they didn't let Vanessa know how disappointed they were, or what they thought of Stuart.

"Hello, Dad, yes I'm fine. No, I can't come this weekend; Stuart's been away on business for three weeks and I'm exhausted. I've been immersing myself in my work and the children have been making great progress. I'm sorry you're disappointed, but at least I have some great news for you and mum; I'm going to have a baby, in seven .months. We're celebrating with Stuart's friends over the weekend so I can't come up, but thanks for the offer anyway. Love to Mum, bye.

A couple of weeks later: "Sorry, I know I'm late getting back to you. I'm fine now, although my ribs are a bit sore from falling down a couple of stairs on Friday after our friends left. Stuart is playing golf with Simon; it seems they planned it a while ago. No, I don't need to go to hospital. I don't need treatment. Thanks for the offer of a weekend break - I'll bear it in mind. Love to Mum, bye."

Chapter 5

Andy curled up tightly on his bedroom floor. Sleep eluded him as his frustration grew. Impractical escape plans whirled around in his brain. The replica of his flat was no consolation for the misery he felt. He was preoccupied with the stark, desolation outside and by being powerless to extricate himself physically or mentally from this unwelcome situation; it was the first time, as an adult, that he had been unable to find a way out of his difficulties.

To his astonishment an unfamiliar scene seeped into his thoughts. It can't have been a memory, although that's how it felt. He was a few days old and being carried home from hospital in the warm, safe, arms of his mother. Once safely inside the comfort of their luxurious home, Vanessa lovingly placed her tiny son into his new and expensive crib. Andrew (his parents' chosen name) immediately began to cry, wanting to be back in his mother's arms. Vanessa was just about to take him out of the crib when Stuart bellowed "leave him alone! Come and sit with me." Startled, Vanessa joined her husband on the sofa, leaving a subtle distance between them. He hurriedly moved closer and pinned Vanessa down with one hand while the other pulled her skirt up and his hand pushed between her thighs.

"I've arranged for Gerry and Simon to come round later and I want to take you to bed; it's been a long time," Stuart said.

"I'm feeling tired, Stuart, and I've got to feed Andrew before I can have a quick nap," said Vanessa.

"I'll cancel the rotten arrangement, shall I? Our most treasured friends and you're incapable of showing your appreciation of their exquisite presents. You just care about yourself, and that thing in the crib!" he shouted. Without further ado, Stuart picked up his keys, threw his coat over his shoulder, and left the house without a word.

He eventually returned home during the early hours of the morning, falling asleep on the sofa, still fully dressed in his expensive clothes, expressly chosen to impress the hospital staff. Had he taken the trouble to search out his wife, he would have found her sitting up in bed, her eyes red and swollen, with Andrew suckling her breast. The following morning, Stuart was up at dawn, showered and dressed, and, with his bag packed, left on a business trip to Europe without seeing Vanessa or his son. Vanessa heard her husband moving about and lay, petrified, in their bed, quietly praying Andrew wouldn't cry and provoke another outburst before Stuart left the house.

Alone, isolated from her parents and friends, Vanessa cried for most of the day and dearly wanted Stuart to return early from his trip, the loving and romantic husband she knew he could be; but he never did. Vanessa was to discover that she was at the beginning of a long, frequently cruel, journey, which would have far-reaching consequences for her and her son.

As a toddler, Andrew played happily with the vast array of expensive toys his parents provided. He always played alone, never experiencing the company of other children or learning that it was more fun to play with friends; for Andrew, playing alone was the norm. He loved his mother and, for the most part, had her all to himself, but his happiness was quickly squashed when his father reappeared from his business trips. By the time he was four, Andrew was adept at interpreting the signs of his father's impending return. The usual entertainments, created especially for him by his mother, would cease and be replaced with vigorous domestic activity. Sumptuous meals would be planned and prepared, the table was lavishly set with the best china and cutlery. A spray of flowers added a discreet air of romance. "Daddy's coming home," however, would also mean the smiles leaving his mother's face and her body stiffening. Just before his father's arrival, Andrew would be washed, changed, and put to bed with military precision. He eventually came to realise that he would never be rescued when his father was at home. He learned not to cry and to put up with whatever discomfort he was in.

He was a little older when he realised that, following one of his father's outbursts, his mother would give a little yelp if he jumped onto her lap. This was generally preceded by an accusation that his mother had failed to comply with an instruction. His father seemed to enjoy criticising her housework, and smirked when she tried hard to appease him. From the luxury of his bedroom, Andrew heard his mother's screams when she was being assaulted; the bedclothes never managed to muffle her cries. As time went by, Andrew found it harder to remain in his bedroom while his father's fists rained blows on his mother's feeble body, but she never allowed him to intervene, fearing that he would exacerbate the situation and be injured himself. He had no option but to stay in his room from where he listened to the commotion that went on until his father ran out of steam and fell asleep.

The next morning Stuart always avoided the consequences of his violent outbursts by leaving the house before the others were awake. The residue of each visit was an atmosphere of prolonged dullness, but Vanessa and Andrew never discussed its cause. On his next return, Stuart would shower Vanessa with expensive gifts and the couple would be demonstratively affectionate, but this always excluded Andrew. His hatred of his father, and his impotence in respect of his mother's vulnerability, created tremendous anxieties that stayed with him far beyond his childhood.

Andrew was exactly 10 years and 240 days old when his mother dropped the bombshell. The pair were having what was traditionally called their "special time", meaning that Stuart was away on business leaving them free to share tender, loving, moments. These times never compensated for the times when her affection was withdrawn, but Andrew revelled in them nevertheless. Vanessa said it had been a joint decision to send him to boarding school; "You're a little behind with your school work and this excellent school will redress the balance. "But she failed to convince Andrew who knew the plan was his father's idea, even when Vanessa defended Stuart saying, "Your father has gone to considerable lengths to secure you a place at such a prestigious school." There would be no arbitration. Andrew knew that any negotiation with his father would be futile. The decision had been Stuart's and Vanessa was obliged to accept it. In any case Andrew had no real communication with his father and dissent on his part would be likely to have detrimental consequences for his mother. His grandparents, Frederick and Jean, had told him that they were always there should he need to speak to them, and even gave him an expensive mobile telephone. There was one occasion when he thought of contacting them. His bicycle wheel had been punctured, but his mother quickly resolved the situation by taking the wheel to a repair shop. Vanessa had been greatly relieved to have rescued the situation without having to visit her parents' home and attempt to hide her bruises. Subsequently, Jean and Frederick knew that Stuart made pretty sure that Andrew had few opportunities for open conversations with them, and Andrew didn't understand that their offers of help extended to his emotional well being.

It was just a couple of days prior to Andrew being whisked off to his new school when Vanessa told her parents about it. Any earlier attempt would have invited discussion and revealed her impotence in the matter. The change of school, and his father's failure to speak with him had, Andrew was sure, resulted from the recent Parents' Evening at which his parents had met his primary school teacher, Mr. Collins. Stuart made a point of attending all his son's school events as they gave him an opportunity to lord it over those to whom he considered himself superior. Of course, there were many who saw beyond the facade, including Mr. Collins who, during their meeting, raised the subject of Andrew's academic and sporting attainments, the latter being more praiseworthy than the former.

However, Mr. Collins said, "It's Andrew's behaviour that concerns me most." He told Vanessa and Stuart that their son was a quiet boy who had few friends and was sometimes bullied by other children. Of course, he said, the teachers monitored the situation. What worried the staff the most was Andrew's swiftness to rage, sometimes triggered by very minor incidents. Mr. Collins did not let the couple know he'd been reluctant to raise his concerns with them, preferring to let Andrew articulate his problems for himself. As this strategy had proved fruitless, his only other option had been to talk things over with Vanessa and Stuart. Stuart listened to the teacher and thanked him for his advice and support, but privately he felt humiliated.

Andrew only had a couple of weeks to reconcile himself to the boarding school plan before he was whisked away by his father, who made no attempt to hide his keenness. It was the school's policy that potential pupils should view the facilities and meet senior staff prior to admission. However, Stuart managed to bypass this process. He realised the policy "was sensible but, with my heavy business commitments and my wife's nervous disposition, it simply can't be done." Once again, Stuart's manipulative tactics had resulted in him getting his own way. Although the school was relatively near, Stuart used the awkwardness of the route, his business commitments, and his desire to avoid disrupting Andrew's education, as reasons for visiting his son just once each term. The consolation offered to Andrew was that his long school holidays would be dedicated to his pleasure but, pointedly, his father was never there. His grandparents sent him numerous, exciting, parcels, and their visits were marked on his calendar as days to relish. Frederick and Jean were fun to be with. Usually taking advantage of the countryside, they planned long, adventurous days, which delighted Andrew. Before departing they hugged each, often their faces wet with tears.

The school consisted of a series of large, red brick, buildings. Andrew found the buildings and the extensive grounds quite forbidding and once ensconced in his designated house and dormitory, he seldom left their confines. School rules prohibited leaving the premises without permission. Andrew never found this restriction bothersome as the world outside held no interest for him. Most often, parents, or friends' parents, arranged out of school activities for their sons and their friends, but this was not so for Andrew, who considered his confinement to be imprisonment. His seven school years were often desolate, lacking the intimacy most of the boys enjoyed. He had one fairly close friend, Gordon, with whom he shared some recreational time, but Gordon was a popular boy who had many, competing, social and sporting interests. The friends did play for the same rugby team, occasionally representing their school. Andrew found the physical side of the game exhilarating and it alleviated his emotional pain to some degree. Afterwards, in the relative comfort of their room, the pair analysed the game whilst indulging in contraband cigarettes and the occasional bottle of wine that Gordon had managed to smuggle in. Andrew loved the luxury of his friend's undivided attention and his tales about his fabulous family life. Gordon did wonder why his friend never reciprocated, but he was a wise friend and he knew not to delve. Andrew had learned caution and he was unable and unwilling to bare his soul or to discuss his family's complexities. Besides, secretiveness had long since become his mainstay, fearful that loose talk could have unpleasant repercussions for his mother and, to a lesser extent, him. Andrew never told anyone how the alarm bells tolled during the stilted telephone conversations with his mother when he tried to find out how she was. He began to dread these calls and was always grateful for any opportunity not to take them. His father never bothered to telephone, choosing instead to send the occasional post card from wherever he happened to be travelling.

Schoolmasters responsible for Andrew's care and education, were acutely aware that he was uncommunicative and that family matters weighed heavily on him, but they were never able to coax him into unburdening himself. The persistent anxiety about his mother, and the damage to his self-esteem caused by his father's insensitive bullying, ensured that Andrew did not shine academically and won no prizes.

At the end of his school years, Andrew's father made it perfectly clear that he would not be returning home. Stuart was embarrassed by his son's poor results and he certainly didn't want his friends to know how much Andrew had disgraced him. He would, of course, fund his move to independence, but that would be the end of his financial contributions; he'd "done it for far too long." Andrew was well aware of the futility of asking his mother to intercede; he was out of the family home, and that was that. Away from his father's influence Andy felt able to broach the subject of her marriage with his mother, but it was to no avail. She would try to quieten him with a dismissive wave of the hand and comments like "he's not so bad. "If Andy persisted, his mother would dissolve into tears and seek refuge in her bedroom.

Chapter 6

It took a little while for Andy's eyes to adjust to the dim lighting. Having given up on sleep as an escape from his unpleasant thoughts, he decided to visit the lounge for a coffee. He was startled to find a stranger whose full figure was snuggled tightly into a large, padded, chair. "Hello, I'm Jeremy. Jeff said we had a new arrival, but I was beginning to doubt him," said Jeremy. The lounge was a comfortable space, an oasis in an otherwise vast, comfortless building. Jeremy and Andy talked in hushed tones, as though reluctant to create an echo that would invade from their cosy cocoon.

"I'm just about to finish the late shift, can I get you anything?" Jeremy offered.

"No, I'm fine."

"How are you getting along? I know the strangeness can be exhausting at first, and I'm glad to have this opportunity to meet you without the hustle and bustle of the daytime crew. It appears, from the little I know about you, that I knew your granddad, Frederick. A grand chap. We taught at the same grammar school for several years. Didn't know your grandmother so well. We only met a couple of times. Was her name Janice?"

"No, Jean," replied Andy.

"Frederick worried about your mother a great deal, but he was always a bit guarded; probably anxious not to be disloyal."

Jeremy went on to explain how saddened Frederick was by the absence of a solid relationship with his daughter and grandson, and how he'd frequently tried to persuade Vanessa to leave Stuart and make a fresh start, maybe nearer to her parents so they could be available to help when necessary. Whenever he seemed to be prevailing, Stuart managed to talk Vanessa out of leaving.

"I gathered that the damage to their daughter's life was a heavy burden to both of them. Loved you, they did," said Jeremy.

"I never realised."

"Right, as I said, a grand couple. I realise this life is vastly different from your previous one. May I suggest that if you relax and learn as much as you can, you'll be fine. I'm off to my room. Not so keen on the late shift. You tend to get a lot of drunks wanting to pull a beautiful blond, or depressives looking for enlightenment. I'd like to throw them in the bin, but can't bring myself to do it."

Wandering back to his room, Andy reflected on Jeremy's attitude to his work, and doubted that he would be capable of the same generosity. He'd been comforted by Jeremy's gentle manner and trusted his judgment, perhaps because of what he'd said about his family. Andy discovered that he was exhausted and sleep no longer eluded him; he slept for several hours.

"Where have you been?" asked Jeff.

"Around and about."

"Got some work for you. It's a simple *request*. The discussions took place earlier and, as you weren't around, the team decided you should be able to manage it. If you need help, just ask."

"Good for them." Andy was fully aware that a *request* had arrived earlier but had chosen to ignore the rumblings of the molten rock in favour of more time in bed. With nothing else to do, he decided to tackle the contents of the papers thrust into his hand by Jeff,

The *request* was for two tickets for that evening's football game between England and Brazil. Andy's glumness and lack of interest (he was a rugby man) gave rise to a solution that appealed to him, despite being a little macabre. He would arrange for the fans' deaths and they'd be able to watch the game from a prime location. He chose his plan with a view to avoiding criticism and to make the most of his limited expertise. Jeff's comment about it being a "simple *request*" had annoyed him, but he was obliged to consult him. With insufferable smugness Jeff had advised him to make an approach to the Sports Department. His advice paid off and two tickets were dropped en route from the printers to the stadium. "Fell from the skies!" shouted one happy recipient, adding a promise to be good.

With his task completed, Andy joined his colleagues except for Jeremy who had not yet arrived. He helped himself to a coffee. Single living, and a large measure of arrogance, meant he didn't consider whether anyone else might fancy one. It wasn't long before they were joined by a slightly flustered Jeremy who apologised for being late and offered to get coffees for everyone.

"By the way, I'm ordering fish and chips tonight. Anyone fancy joining me?" Jeremy asked.

Andy didn't enjoy being part of a team; having colleagues was repellent to him. Moreover, his workplace reminded him of his claustrophobic school days. His new existence was similar to that of Dave and Joe, his old friends - a life-style he despised. With a rueful smile, Andy determined that his previous life experience would enable him to mould his new circumstances into something more to his liking. Most of the team had broken up for the night leaving Jeremy and Andy by themselves. Jeremy politely put his newspaper, The Nirvana Chronicle down when Andy spoke to him.

"Have you been here long?" he asked.

"Yes, quite some time. I could have moved on but, having discussed my options with the Influencing Team, I decided to stay. Are you having something to eat?"

"I'll eat in my room later. The food ordering machine is awesome; such a varied selection."

"We had to vary the menus to accommodate the palates of our younger members. My fondness remains with the more traditional foods of my youth, particularly a roast dinner which is often unavailable due to high demand. Would you like another coffee?"

"Yes...thanks," said Andy.

Jeremy said his earthly existence had been a simple one, built around the pleasure he derived from the English language. He'd chosen to be an English teacher and it was while he was working in a local grammar school that he'd met Andy's grandfather, Frederick. Jeremy was a confirmed bachelor. He had enjoyed caring for his parents until their deaths which had been several years apart. He enjoyed the freedom of his single life which allowed him to pursue his sporting interests - football, table tennis, and crown green bowling - as much as he wanted. He also enjoyed placing the occasional bet and rounding his evenings off with a decent meal and a few single, malt whiskies. He had remained in his childhood home until his death which, like his life, was peaceful and unstressed.

By the way," Andy asked, "how do I go about getting new clothes and arranging for laundry?"

"You need to see Peggy," Jeremy told him.

"Who?"

"Peggy. She works in Reception, just through the door opposite the molten rock. It's signed, you can't miss it. It's too late to catch her now, better try first thing in the morning."

Andy suspected that Jeremy always wore the same clothes; comfortable corduroy trousers, plain shirts, and a homely cardigan with pockets stretched out of shape by his broad fists.

Chapter 7

The following morning, as advised, Andy went in search of Reception, checking the contents of his desk on his way. Checking his desk had nothing to do with the possible arrival of ***requests***; he was suspicious about Jeff possibly having a rummage and he wanted the reassurance that no tampering had occurred.

He had woken up feeling agitated and in no mood to be questioned or instructed by anyone. It was obvious to him that his colleagues had no idea how important his father was. He thought they would become more respectful when they found out.

"Yes?" queried Peggy.

"I'm Andy and I've been told you could help me get some new clothes and sort out some laundry for me."

"Who told you that?"

"Not sure. I'm new and not familiar with peoples' names yet."

"So you're just up?"

"Yes, been here a couple of days, had to wait...."

"Don't need your history, lad, " Peggy interrupted, "just your name. I have to fill out a chitty. Can't say how long it'll take; been inundated with people moaning all morning; always moaning, never a thank you."

Andy thought about the sign in the Social Security office, took a seat, and considered the similarities. A big difference, however, was that there was only one person ahead of him.

"Next!" called Peggy.

The man sitting beside Andy stood up and walked the few feet to Peggy's desk. She didn't ask him for personal details. In fact, she didn't even look at him.

"I'd like a transfer."

"Where to, Alistair?"

"Medical"

"Fill in the form."

When he'd completed the form, Alistair left.

"That man's a bloody nuisance; he's worked in nearly every department. He thinks he's capable of being a brain surgeon, but he can't empty a bin bag without making a mess. Wherever he works I get complaint after complaint. He's got to work somewhere, but I don't know where. If I approach The Medical Team they'll think I've lost my marbles. I'll suggest they find him a minor role and then everyone will be happy.....until the next time. Can't sack him, he hasn't done anything wrong. Besides, where would he go, no Big Issues on sale here," finished Peggy.

Having done everything required, Andy left Reception and returned to his desk where he was joined by Jeff who strutted towards him, cutting off his conversation with Sarah in mid flow.

"Glad to see you. Thought I'd never get away from her," said Jeff.

"Who?" asked Andy?

"Doesn't matter. I believe you've been to Reception?"

Jeff began to tell him about Peggy. Andy tried to stop him by walking away, but that didn't discourage Jeff. He simply trailed after him, continuing to tell him all about Peggy. She'd been married to Harold for over thirty years when, ten years ago, they were killed in a car crash and assigned to different departments on the Holding Station. Harold had been a merchant seaman all his working life, and had spent very little time at home. When his captain asked for volunteers to remain aboard while they were in harbour, Harold was always first to offer. Peggy never questioned his explanation that there was nobody else available. Retirement posed problems for Harold but he never complained about missing the camaraderie of his shipmates and the freedoms they enjoyed. Harold found retirement claustrophobic. It wasn't long after he retired that Harold crashed his car, head on, into a tree, killing Peggy and himself instantly. After arriving at the Holding Station, Harold seized his first opportunity to ask Barrie to send Peggy and himself to different postings. Peggy never thought anything was amiss until she overheard a chance remark from her hairdresser, Tracy, who was one of only a handful of people able to move about freely. Outraged, she stormed over to the management department and demanded to see Barrie. Barrie told her she'd had no reason to deny Harold's request for a position in The Fashion Department. Peggy argued, pointing out that Harold knew nothing whatever about fashion. Her case was hopeless, however, and her efforts futile. In the end she had to accept defeat and apologise for her aggressiveness. She was also embarrassed that everyone knew about Harold's desire to be separated from her. For some time Peggy rarely left the Reception area. She refused to see Tracy, "that cow of a hairdresser" and, consequently, the appearance of her hair deteriorated.

At this point in Jeff's narrative, the molten rock erupted giving Andy a chance to retrieve a fax and break away from him. Peter was pleased to see Andy working and beckoned to him, not realising Andy's sole purpose had been to dislodge Jeff.

"How are you today, Andy? I'm sorry I didn't have a chance to catch up with you yesterday," Peter apologised.

"I'm good, settling in fine," replied Andy.

"We thought you could try something a little more challenging, more meat on the bone, so to speak. Most *requests* are original, meaning they've come from people previously unknown to us. On the odd occasion a *request* is repeated, we are reluctant to change the original worker - as was the case some time ago when a child made many requests for snow and Sarah stayed with it throughout. Do you get my drift?"

Peter seemed unaware of his pun and Andy decided to hide his amusement.

"This *request* came in earlier, "Peter went on, "and, as you were with Peggy, the team had a look at it and agreed that you should be able to deal with the issues involved. Look it over and, if you feel able, carry on."

Peter had barely finished speaking when a bright green light on his desk started flashing. He seemed flustered and, gathering up some papers, he left immediately. In Andy's opinion the *request* was unimportant so, leaving it to one side, he headed for the lounge where he was joined by Sarah.

"Did you manage to sort out your laundry and new clothes?" she asked Andy.

"Not really sure; she filled out a chitty and gave me a copy, so I presume something will be sorted out."

"Shouldn't hold your breath."

They both smiled at this as breath, or the lack of it, no longer mattered to them.

Chapter 8

Suddenly, without any explanation, Andy returned to his room for lunch and a nap. He considered his decision to retreat was his own affair and didn't call for any discussion. For quite some time he lounged on his bed considering the extensive menu at his disposal. The food provided was far better than anything he could have prepared for himself, and it was free and ready-made. Andy thought about the other people he'd met since arriving at the Holding Station. He didn't think they were his sort of people and couldn't see them providing the entertainment he needed. Andy had never coped well with disappointment or frustration and so his present predicament left him depressed and dispirited. He cheered up a little when he resolved to change things for himself, although he was cross with himself for not making the decision sooner.

His central idea was to expand his horizons, to escape his immediate, stifling, situation. After all, there were other departments; hadn't he spoken to someone in the Sports Department? Harold had been assigned to Fashion, Alistair to Medical, it was reasonable to assume there were many others, all full of people. He needed to explore further afield; to search out his own kind. Andy felt much better now that he was making plans. The idea of moving about freely was liberating in itself, and he tried to maintain his optimism by shelving his planning for the time being and ordering himself a special lunch after which he slept for an hour or two.

He woke up refreshed and returned to his desk where he noticed the *request* he'd neglected to deal with. It was marked "Urgent" and called for someone's electricity supply to be reconnected. Andy's groan brought Sarah to his side.

"What's up?" she asked

"It's this bloody **request** for an electricity reconnection; do people really have their supply cut off?"

"Yes, sometimes. It's a good idea to use the viewer - that's it, on the corner of your desk - then you can see the situation for yourself. You can ask anyone for advice, but for more difficult problems it would be wise to go to Peter; he's the most experienced. I'll leave you to it. Don't hesitate to ask for help if you need it."

Andy had been unaware of the viewer because he'd ignored Jeff's advice to familiarise himself with the contents of his desk. When tinkering with the controls failed to do anything more than produce a stream of white, electrical, flashes, Andy switched the viewer off and joined Sarah in the lounge.

"How's it going?" she asked

"Great....up and running."

"I knew you were a clever chap, that you wouldn't have any problems."

Andy sank into an arm chair, cradling his coffee and pondering his future plans. Being alone with Sarah gave him the ideal opportunity to quiz her about the wilderness outside.

"Do you ever go to other departments?" Andy asked.

"Occasionally, but only for special events; it's rare for this team to accept invitations- we're not a very sociable group."

"Do you need permission to go out and about?"

"No, but you need a good reason, usually an emergency. At the end of reception, by the way out, is the Destination Book. It's where you log your destination and journey time each time you go out. It's tatty, from age, not wear and tear, because we seldom use it. Not logging your trips properly is taken very seriously. Anyway, you'll get a chance to see further afield tomorrow. We're all going to the launch of the new women's uniforms in the Fashion Department.

Chapter 9

The following morning, Andy discovered that a note from Peggy had been pushed under his door, letting him know that his new clothes and his laundry were all ready for him. Without further ado, Andy swaggered over to Reception, eager to take possession of his new clothes.

"Hi, Peggy. Fantastic, I believe my clothes are ready for collection?"

"You'll have to come back later. No time now."

"Come on, Peggy, surely you can find a minute for me?"

"No...I can't."

"OK, what would be the best time to call back?"

"Dunno," said Peggy, "Just keep trying."

Thwarted, and with little else to do, Andy spent a while tuning his screen before going back to see Peggy. This time she was less flustered and handed him his clothes with a good grace.

By-passing his desk, he went directly to his room, intent on getting ready for the night ahead. Bored of waiting for the adventure to begin, he mopped up some time in trying on his new, stylish, possessions and wondered why he thought his new clothes would impress others when, as a handsome young man, he could let his looks speak for him.

At the start of the evening his colleagues met in the lounge. They'd all made an effort with their appearance and Andy was startled by the appearance of the smartly dressed group. In line with the regulations they all recorded the details of their outing in the Destination Book. Andy was very excited when, for the first time since his arrival at the Earthly Team headquarters, he found himself outside. The bright horizon was masked by wispy bands of white, grey, and black clouds sometimes intermingled, and sometimes in neat layers. Realising that

Andy was uncertain in his unaccustomed surroundings, Sarah took his elbow and gently steered him along as they followed a little behind Jeremy, Jeff, and Peter. Andy was unaware of Sarah's kind intentions. If he'd realised what she was doing he would have been furious at the slight to his masculinity. During their walk, Sarah painted a picture of the fun and frivolity he could expect because of all the trendy and exciting people who worked in the Fashion Department. Andy wasn't listening, however, because he was trying to work out how the three men in front were finding their way so confidently. The terrain seemed hostile to Andy. It was in stark contrast to the huge, iron, building they'd left behind, where their earthly existence had been so meticulously recreated.

It wasn't far to the Fashion Department, but Andy knew he'd be unable to find his own way; the pathway had no discernible features or landmarks, and certainly no signposts. Andy had no idea how the men in front were navigating, and this failure threw him into a bad temper which distracted him from noticing the elegant entrance and hallway at the Fashion Department. He was jogged back to reality when Jeff introduced him to those tasked with welcoming guests. In that moment he was grateful to Peggy for providing him with his beautiful Paul Smith suit. Jeff gave him his customary assessment of everyone there, unable to keep excitement out of his voice. Andy thought he was probably too impressed by the guest list. This wasn't too surprising as there were a few people with royal ancestry, some famous musicians, and some sporting "greats".

None of these celebrities impressed Andy who had no interest in their achievements and no desire to spend time with them. He did notice a tall, bearded, man, unkempt by Andy's standards, whom he thought he recognised, although he couldn't be sure. Jeff made no mention of the man and Andy didn't take the matter further.

He sidled away from Jeff and walked, truculently, to the back of the room. Both Sarah and Jeremy tried to encourage him to mingle, but their efforts were in vain. The evening was drawing to an end and the crowd was dwindling when Andy was struck by a woman whom he hadn't glimpsed before. She had been hidden by a cluster of men which wasn't surprising given how beautiful she was. Andy had just about mustered the confidence to approach her when Jeremy caught his arm and nodded towards the exit; they were heading back as "no doubt there'll be a host of *requests* accumulating." With no other choice he was obliged to leave, his frustrations undiminished. The ritual of The Destination Book did nothing to improve Andy's mood.

Chapter 10

Back in the comfort of the Earthly Team's rooms Andy persuaded Sarah to have a coffee with him, and even offered to make it. He led their conversation in the direction of the woman who'd caught his eye.

"That's Alicia. She's worked in the Fashion Department for quite some time. Most of the women complain that the designs are frumpish and accuse her of deliberately producing designs that only she could look good in. You've probably noticed Alicia would look stunning in a sack - and "sack" is what the uniforms are generally called."

"They're not so bad," said Andy.

"You think! Seems to me they're modelled on M&S or the Halifax designs."

"Why don't people complain?"

"There's no point," said Sarah, "she's popular with management and they pay no attention to our complaints."

"Why don't the men have to wear uniforms?"

"Peter managed to persuade the Influencing Team, with significant support from Barrie, that Jeremy would not easily adapt to such a drastic change, having worn his own "uniform" for so long. The exemption was extended to all the men on the team, leaving me as the only one having to wear a uniform," Sarah sighed.

Once in the privacy of his room, Andy tried to fathom out how his colleagues had found their way to the Fashion Department. He was depressed by what he saw as his incarceration. He had no real freedom of movement, only being able to move about in strictly controlled circumstances. For the time being, his only liberty lay in his fantasies about Alicia. The next day he was up and about early as he planned to complete the *request* for reconnection of fuel which would give him time to pursue Alicia. Grabbing a coffee on the way to his desk, he noted the others were already working!

Balancing on the two back legs of his chair, coffee in hand, he set about his task, motivated entirely by self interest. The pictures on his screen were poor, but showed him a young woman who was surrounded by several children, all wrapped in blankets protecting them from the chill of a brisk winter's day. Staggered by the lack of heating and dismayed by the mother's financial ineptitude, Andy concluded that his father's assertions were correct; they "fritter it away on bingo and drinking" was his attitude to people experiencing financial difficulties. Taking his father's view as his own basis for inaction, Andy believed that the young woman's distress was self-indulgent self pity and that she was the author of her own misfortunes. He had little sympathy for the family's plight and once again left the matter in abeyance. He went away to enjoy his dreaming about the delectable Alicia, and later on met up with Jeremy who had resumed his late shift.

"How are you today? Did you enjoy yourself last night?" Jeremy asked him.

"Not bad. It was refreshing to get away from here for a bit. Couldn't get my bearings though, and I wondered how I could find my way around if I need to go out again."

"Shouldn't worry too much about that. There's seldom any need to go out as everything we need is here, conveniently to hand."

"But," Andy persisted, "there must be some occasions when it's necessary to go out alone."

"Not really, maybe on odd occasions when the computer and telephone lines are down and information's needed from other departments, but Information Technology is pretty good and they generally repair things quickly and reliably, making journeys between departments largely unnecessary."

Andy tried again.

"Do people call, on each other, say socially and without warning?"

"Not really. Staff are usually too busy to make impromptu social calls, and it's not encouraged."

"Not encouraged!" exclaimed Andy, "Is there a rule?"

"No but it's, well, frowned upon, viewed as a distraction."

"Who by?"

"The powers that be."

Their conversation came to an abrupt end when Peter appeared and interrupted them. By this time, however, Andy had realised he wouldn't get any further with Jeremy on the particular matter of moving between departments.

Chapter 11

"Andy, are you dealing with Sheila? enquired Peter.
"Who?"

"Sheila."

"Can't say that I am."

"Your name's on the *request* form."

"Is that the woman who's having problems with her electricity?"

"Yes."

"Well, then, yes I am. It's nearly sorted- should be finished off fairly soon."

"You've had this for a couple of days," Peter said sternly.

"I know, but it's been a little tricky."

"Why didn't you ask for help?"

"Didn't seem necessary; as I say, it's nearly sorted."

Having said his piece, Peter left.

"A bit sharp," said Andy, looking to Jeremy for support. He was drastically off course. Jeremy had gone back to reading the Nirvana Chronicle without uttering another syllable. With a measure of insolence, Andy slowly finished his coffee and moved back to his desk. In no time at all he was reporting his success to Peter, intimating that he was "at a loss to see what all the fuss" had been about. He explained that he'd simply contacted the Weather Department who arranged for a couple of youths playing football to break a window just moments before gusts of wind blew through it and sent the paperwork from the electricity office whirling about. When the papers were gathered together, Sheila's was on top of the pile and, following a couple of 'phone calls, her supply was soon reconnected.

Andy drifted through the next few weeks, picking up the odd *request*, but nothing too taxing. As for the rest of the team, they were far too busy to pay him much attention and far from eager to do anything about it. He didn't appear to be avoiding his colleagues. He was neither friendly nor unfriendly, merely preoccupied. He wanted a valid reason for contacting Alicia and wouldn't allow anyone or anything to distract him for long.

Andy was at his desk when he saw Peter making his way purposefully towards him. "What does that bastard want now?" he wondered. "Something for you to look into. It's not crucial in the scheme of things, but it needs to be dealt with quickly as I've held onto it for a few days. As you weren't about, again, for our morning discussion, we decided that this was one for you; shall I leave it with you?"

"Yes, er, thanks," said Andy. Peter returned to his desk and continued with his work without registering Andy's relative politeness. Andy's moods were variable and this sort of thing meant very little. Andy glanced at the papers Peter had handed him and was about to put them aside in favour of lunch when he saw it was a *request* for a wedding dress. He was stung into action and immediately switched on his monitor and saw Jane, crying at the prospect of not getting the wedding dress of her childhood dreams.

Chapter 12

Had his luck finally changed? The wedding dress would be his reason for contacting Alicia but it would require care to manufacture a meeting without being found out. His first move would be to telephone Alicia to ask her for advice about the dress. He rummaged around until he found a dog-eared telephone directory. Opposite Alicia Jennings, Fashion Department was the number, 4543. He waited impatiently until Jeremy came to do his late shift and began reading his newspaper. Undisturbed, but with a trembling hand, he dialled Alicia's number.

"Hello."

"Yes...erm...can I speak to Alicia Jennings please?" Andy asked.

"She's not here just now. She'll be back tomorrow-can I take a message?"

"Thanks, that would be helpful. Could you ask her to ring Andy Goodyear, Earthly Team 47776? By the way, who's speaking?"

"John."

"OK John, would you let her know there's a degree of urgency and I'd be grateful if she could call as soon as possible?"

The next morning he was at his desk before any of his colleagues. Troubled by the lack of response from Alicia. Andy forgot his own advice to be cautious, and dialled Alicia's number once more.

"Is that you, John?"

"Yes."

"It's Andy Goodyear here. Did Alicia get my message?"

"Yes, but she's busy and I can't interrupt her. I'll remind her to call as soon as she's free."

"Cheers."

Andy felt things were not going well, not going his way at all. He huffed and puffed his way to the lounge for a coffee, which he spilled onto his jeans when he stumbled into the chair next to Sarah's. Vexed by his lack of success he marched to his room to change his jeans. He paced the floor, letting his imagination run riot. Eventually he convinced himself that John had deliberately withheld his message because he and Alicia were having an affair or, even worse, they were making fun of him. Annoyed with himself for having invented his own unhappy scenarios, he remained in his room for a while. Then he began to worry that his earlier, brusque, behaviour may have upset some of the others and, after a quick breakfast, and smartening himself up, he went back to his desk, wishing everyone a "good morning" on his way. If he'd hoped to avoid any conversation with them, his hopes were dashed by Jeremy.

"How are you feeling this morning?" Jeremy asked. "You seemed somewhat troubled yesterday. I hope nothing was said to offend you. We're a small team and spend a lot of time together, so it's important we get along with each other."

"Just had a bit of a bad day," Andy said.

"Yes, I understand. It can take time to get accustomed to our unfamiliar environment and routines. From what I gleaned from Frederick's description of your father, you're a lot like him."

"Am I?" Andy wondered. Although he wasn't paying Jeremy his full attention, he was taken aback by his judgement; years ago he had decided his father was an ogre and not to be emulated in any way. However, Jeremy's evaluation was nothing compared to his anxiety over Alicia telephoning him. The whole day dragged by, and Jeremy was about to begin his late shift, when Alicia finally called.

"Can I speak to Andy Goodyear, please?"

"This is Andy Goodyear. Am I speaking to Alicia?"

"Yes."

"I was at your soiree the other night. I was the handsome young man wearing a grey, Paul Smith, suit. Do you remember me?"

"No, I'm not really sure that I do. How can I help you?"

"I've been trying to get an exquisite wedding dress, but I don't have the foggiest where to start. I hoped you would be able to help me."

"I have several brochures which you might find helpful. John will get them to you tomorrow."

"That's too late. I need them now. The ***request*** is urgent so I'll get directions and nip across for them."

"No, that's not advisable as you're not management - or are you?"

"No, I'm not, yet!"

"I've got a few bits and pieces to finish here," Alicia said, and then I'll bring the brochures over to you. See you shortly."

Not wanting Jeremy to see what he was doing, Andy replaced the receiver gently then slipped quietly into his room where he hurriedly washed his dirty dishes. The dirty clothes he hadn't passed on to Peggy were pushed under the mattress, and some clean ones he'd left scattered about were tidied away properly. When he'd finished he surveyed his efforts with pride and thought Jeremy was right to comment that he was like his father. After all, hadn't he always instilled a sense of pride in him. A knock on the door made his pulse race, but it was only Jeremy.

"Alicia has the brochures you urgently required," Jeremy announced.

"Ask her to bring them into my room so she can go through them with me without any interruptions."

"Not allowed, old chap. Besides, there's only me in the office and I can make myself scarce."

Seeing Alicia in the brighter lights of the Earthly Team office, Andy was even more struck by her beauty. Swiftly, and with no small talk, Alicia set about showing Andy the most impressive dresses, adding her opinions about suitability for spring weddings. Alicia refused all offers of refreshments and wasted no time in returning to her department when she'd finished examining the brochures. Typically, Andy reacted badly to Alicia's lack of interest in him, fazed about feeling sorry for himself. Meanwhile the situation regarding the ***request*** had moved on. Jane was still upset over her wedding dress, but her fiancé was making things worse. Graham had explained that his bonus payment was destined to repay his gambling debts. He suggested a much quieter wedding celebration with just a few friends and a meal at MacDonald's afterwards. He tried to console her by saying they could have extras paid for out of her salary. Graham's proposals rendered the wedding dress, that Jane had told her friends would be exquisite, completely redundant. Graham's new plan couldn't have been any more different from Jane's and she continued being angry and upset in turn.

Andy believed that most weddings were unnecessarily costly affairs and so his sympathies lay firmly with Graham. Consequently, he planned to extradite "the poor sod" from his awful situation. Andy enthusiastically arranged for an email to be sent to all the employees of Graham's firm, an engineering company, advertising a job in Saudi Arabia. The contract would be for two years and only single accommodation was available. Graham thought the job could provide the answer to his financial difficulties, and he applied successfully; within a few days the job was his. As he anticipated, breaking his news to Jane was far from easy. "Tears and tantrums" he told his workmates. Nevertheless, he had made his decision; he would put himself straight financially while doing work that interested him. At his raucous leaving party, Graham's friends unanimously agreed that if she truly loved him, Jane would wait for a couple of years. This was not how Jane viewed the situation, however, and, feeling humiliated, she terminated their relationship

Andy considered the outcome a success and he could barely hide his smugness when passing the completed paperwork back to Peter. Sometime later, and quite by chance, Andy learned that Jane had married when the molten rock gushed a "thank you" through to the team. With a nonchalant shrug he muttered "Probably Sarah."

With **requests** dwindling after the pre-Christmas deluge, Andy could concentrate on finding a way to meet up with Alicia. He preferred to meet her on her home territory so that he could gain some insight into her situation, especially with regard to John. He spent solitary days in his room working out a plan of action, emerging occasionally to minimise his colleagues' curiosity and to forestall well-intentioned visits. Andy was growing in confidence, convinced that it would be relatively easy to coax Sarah into giving him the information he would need.

Chapter 13

Andy was at his desk, a rarity during the dull days after Christmas, when Jeff came and stood beside him. Andy groaned inwardly. Jeff was irritatingly persistent and even frank rudeness often failed to deter or discourage him.

"I need to talk to you, Andy. You seem to be a man of the world."

"Don't know about that," said Andy, "I'm only twenty-four. Haven't had that much experience."

"I don't know. From what I've heard, you've been rather successful with women." Jeff was remorseless.

"Really? Did you want something as I'm quite busy- got a lot to do."

"It's about Sarah. She's got the hots for me, a bit of a crush. She just won't leave me alone and it's irritating the hell out of me."

"Be careful, Jeff, it may not be such a good idea to mention hell in our circumstances."

"I'm sure it's OK; I've never heard a word about the place."

"Don't you like Sarah? She seems quite nice to me," Andy said.

"I know, but she's not really my type; she's a bit old and not very sexy. I like raunchy women, a bit like Alicia. She's got everything a man could ask for."

"I thought you were around the same age as Sarah?"

"I am, but I don't look my age. I could easily attract a much younger woman. The trouble is there isn't much opportunity around here."

"I think your best plan," Andy said, "is to avoid, as far as possible, all contact with Sarah, and certainly don't make eye contact or engage in small, talk. That should do the trick."

Jeff said he'd give this a try and let Andy know how he got on.

He had no idea how mistaken he was about Sarah. This wasn't very surprising as he paid little attention to what other people wanted or needed. If he'd taken any real interest in Sarah he might have realised she appeared asexual with no desire for intimacy with anyone. Sarah's warmth towards Jeff resulted purely from what she perceived as his need for some stimulation, something to disrupt his dullness.

Sarah's transition into adolescence had been particularly difficult. She'd been under constant pressure from friends and relatives to go on "dates" with local boys. The pressure was greater than it might have been because she was very attractive and had a lovely figure and a lively personality. Admitting her lack of sexuality was not an option as she was reluctant to humiliate her family and to confront the ridicule of her peers. Her lack of romantic experiences grew more problematic as people close to her, of both sexes, made jokes without realising their painful impact on Sarah. She found it increasingly difficult to maintain an appearance of normality and finally decided her only escape was to become a nun. She was almost thirty when she took her final vows. She went to work at an orphanage in Africa, she was glad to be well away from her previous life and really enjoyed her work with the children. The irritations caused by some parts of her disciplined existence were more than outweighed by the joy of spending her days with happy, chattering children. Over the years, Sarah's figure lost much of its sexual allure and became ideal for comforting and cuddling small children. Sarah was pleased to wear the same sort of clothes each day. She'd never wanted to dwell on her physical appearance and was relieved not to have to select her outfit each morning.

It was late evening when Sarah drove the old Volkswagen from the small town back to her convent. It was a dark night and difficult to navigate the unlit road. It was hot and Sarah wound down the car window allowing dust to blow in and obscure her vision. The impact when she hit the large black cow, killed Sarah outright, but the wreckage and Sarah's body weren't found until the following afternoon when buzzards led people to the scene. Sarah's death came as a blow to the children, and she was badly missed. The children honoured her memory by creating a walled garden within the convent which was always known as "Sarah's Garden", even when there was no one left who had known her.

Chapter 14

As Sarah was consumed by her work, drawing her away was proving impossible, and the vital information Andy needed was still beyond his grasp. In desperation he decided to take an ill considered risk. Without telling anyone, and without logging out in the Destinations Book, Andy walked out of the building. Being alone and being outside was intoxicating. He wanted to share the moment and, instinctively, glanced about for Joe and Dave. Andy didn't allow his nervousness to dull the edge of his excitement. His dogged determination carried him forward in pursuit of Alicia. He had no idea about the distances he was covering and, on one occasion, was dismayed to find himself back where he'd started. Once or twice he spotted other people, barely visible through the clouds of white mist surrounding them. He couldn't be sure they wouldn't somehow scupper his plans, so he decided against asking any of them for help. He wandered aimlessly across featureless terrain but somehow, for no discernible reason, he started to be drawn in one particular direction. He gradually became surer footed and, finally, out of the mists appeared a magnificent building with "Fashion Department" emblazoned across the entrance in neon lights.

The journey had been tiring but his fatigue left him in an instant. This success had changed everything. He became more confident and composed, ready to face anything. Without bothering with the huge knocker, Andy pushed open the heavy wooden doors and entered. He didn't bother to sign himself in. He heard voices and walked the length of the hall towards them. The walls were decorated with pictures of different fashions across several centuries. Looking at them made him grateful that he was wearing fashionable clothes that flattered his slender body. The voices led him along a passage into a larger room. There were fabrics and textiles of all descriptions lying about everywhere. Some were on manikins. There were sewing machines ready to create clothes from the cloth. The elegance and brightness of this room contrasted starkly with the Earthly Team's accommodation. Andy spotted Alicia surrounded by several people who appeared preoccupied by the fabric she was holding. He forced his way between Alicia and John.

"Hi, Alicia, I've brought your brochures back, thought you might need them," said Andy.

"That wasn't necessary. We have lots more and, besides, some of these are out of date, but since you're here, I'll introduce you to the team."

"Cheers."

"Sandra, James, and John, this is Andy. I'm afraid our final member, Harold, is busy just now, working hard to meet a deadline."

Taking Alicia's elbow, Andy steered her away from the coffee machine towards the lounge where they sat in the comfort of lime green, bowl chairs. They'd only been there a few moments when John approached them.

"Would you like latte, cappuccino, or filter?" he asked.

"It'd be nice to have latte for a change," Andy replied, "we have no choice, it's Americano or nothing."

"John, would you check Sandra's final design for the new uniforms? If they seem too flamboyant encourage her towards the more traditional design."

Her instructions to John led Andy to believe that Alicia wanted to be alone with him. He wondered why he'd ever considered John to be a threat. He was several years older than Alicia and, although handsome, was rather short. He had deep furrows across his forehead and lacked, seriously lacked, sex appeal. Andy managed to edge his chair nearer to Alicia's until he was able to brush his arm against hers. His excitement rocketed when she didn't pull away from this contact with him. With increasing confidence, Andy touched her knee with his and, once again, she didn't shrink away; Andy was euphoric.

Alicia told him she'd been in the Fashion Department for several years. She'd transferred from the Nirvana Chronicle where she'd worked as a reporter. She found the work there boring and tedious.

She described the monotony of collating statistical data from each Department and analysing it before forwarding it to the Influencing Team. Alicia thought her position at the Chronicle "was not really a proper use of (her) talent" and she was delighted when her transfer to the Fashion Department was agreed. Andy listened in silence, soaking up her every word, sending out the message that she was very important to him. Alicia broke the spell by abruptly announcing that she "needed to get back to work. But she added that she had "enjoyed their time together."

"We'll do it again then," Andy said.

"Maybe, but it's not easy to move between departments."

"I'll find a way, you can be sure of that. I'm not about to stay cooped up in the Earthly Station with that lot!" Andy said.

Before leaving, Andy took his biggest risk, gently kissing Alicia's sensual lips. His kiss wasn't reciprocated but, delightfully, it wasn't rejected.

Fuelled by all his success, Andy confidently embarked on his return journey. Finding the Earthly Station proved far more difficult than finding the Fashion Department had been. The light was more glaring now and he had to shield his eyes with his hands. He was lost and stranded in the seemingly endless, vast, pink, space. His euphoria deserted him and he sank down from sheer exhaustion, all alone in the wilderness. Eventually he was found by Jeremy who helped him back to his room where he slept for twenty-four hours.

Chapter 15

"I heard about your adventure the other night - pretty horrendous. We thought you'd probably need lots of sleep and left you to it. Welcome back, coffee?" Sarah offered.

"Cheers."

"The others are having a short team meeting and left me here to deal with any emergencies."

"How do you find your way around?" asked Andy, "it seems easy for you lot."

"I shouldn't really tell you; you haven't been here long enough, but you seem a decent chap. Just don't let on that it was me who told you. You take the torch to navigate with. When we went over to the Fashion Department, Peter had it. You probably didn't notice because we were some way behind him, and he keeps it up his sleeve so it's less obvious. I think he likes to give the impression that he can manage without it."

"Why on earth didn't someone tell me? I've been locked up in this dump for months, desperate to get out. Who makes the decisions about the bloody torch?"

"Be careful, Andy, it's not sensible to sound off too much. I'm not sure where the torch is kept. It appears to be Peter's responsibility, but I'm not sure why; perhaps he sees himself as being the most senior. He regularly changes the torch's hiding place, making it almost impossible to get hold of it without his knowledge and, I'm telling you, you need a compelling reason to get it."

"Do you know how it works?" Andy asked her.

"No, never had a reason to ask and no one's ever offered to explain. From what I've gathered, however, it would seem to be programmed according to a set of codes. There's usually a list of the codes around here somewhere, but I don't know where they are just now."

"Come on, Sarah, think, think as hard as you can, you're my only hope."

"Start with the top drawer in Peter's desk, that's the most obvious place.

A determined trawl through Peter's desk was successful and he found the codes. With the others busy with their team meeting he was able to photocopy the codes without them knowing. Sarah, too, was unaware of his triumph and he decided not to tell her about it, concerned that she might mention it to someone else and jeopardise his relationship with Alicia. He felt guilty enough to pour Sarah a cup of coffee before retreating to his room to examine the codes. Sitting on his bed with his legs bent so that he could use his knees as a table, he began his task. He soon realised that the codes were as difficult to interpret as an unknown foreign language. He thought the key might have a mathematical source and, for the first time since leaving school, he regretted his lack of academic achievement. His failure to make any progress with the codes disappointed and frustrated him. His powerlessness to do anything about his problems left him feeling wretched. He kept to his room for days at a time, consumed by his need to decode the information concerning the use of the torch. He only emerged for brief periods during which his colleagues avoided him because of his constant irritability.

When Andy decided to end his self-imposed exile, he returned to the team room dishevelled and unshaven. Surprisingly, he asked Peter if there was any work for him to do, and even offered to make coffees for everyone. This improvement in Andy's behaviour was welcome, but his colleagues were not especially interested in his pleasantries, resulting as they did, from his need for their help.

He'd only just sat down when the green light on his desk began to flash. Andy looked to Sarah for advice and was told to "get a move on" as the light meant Barrie wanted to see him in her office.

"How will I get there?" Andy asked.

"Go to Reception and tell Peggy; she'll sort it out, but hurry up, it's not a good idea to keep Barrie waiting."

Chapter 16

"Peggy, I've got to go to Barrie's office. Do you make the arrangements?"

"Yes, I do....and it's a nuisance. It stops me getting on with my proper work and then I get complaints."

She punched information into her computer and told him to wait outside, adding a reminder to make an entry in The Destinations Book. Outside Andy was met by two strangers who introduced themselves as his escort. The three of them walked in silence. This suited Andy because he wanted to focus on how the escorts found their way. When they left him outside Barrie's offices, he was none the wiser. The building reminded him of how scared he'd been on his previous visit. He was far more confident now, believing that he'd accomplished a series of successes and become an asset to the Earthly Team.

The rap on Barrie's door triggered the automatic doors. Barrie, standing behind her desk, greeted Andy with a handshake.

"Good to meet you again, Andy. Our meeting is your six monthly review. Do you remember me telling you that it had been touch and go as to whether you would get a place on the Holding Station?"

"Yes, I do."

"Since your arrival I've been gathering information for this meeting but, before we discuss it, I'd like to know how you've found your first six months."

Andy gave the briefest account of his work to date, claiming that all his involvements had successful conclusions. He was taken aback when Barrie recounted his failures in respect of each of the *requests* he'd dealt with. He was further dismayed that she wanted to look at some factors which she believed had reduced his effectiveness.

"It appears to me that you were insensitive to the facts associated with Sheila's plight," said Barrie.

"Who?" asked Andy

"The family who were living in a cold house. You didn't think their situation was a high priority and delayed your handling of the matter for several days.

Although he thought he was being unfairly criticised, he blamed the poor quality of his screen for not having resolved the family's difficulties more promptly.

"There is also the wedding dress *request*," Barrie continued, "do you honestly think the outcome suited all parties? I'll leave you to think it over. We'll have another chat about your progress in three months time, before we make any decision about your future here."

It would have been sensible to learn more about Barrie's misgivings, and her ideas for addressing them, but Andy was far more interested in his plans to rendezvous with Alicia. To this end, he meant to question his escorts closely on the return journey. So he thanked Barrie for her time and patience before hurrying away, claiming that he was very busy dealing with an emergency.

Chapter 17

There was no one waiting for Andy and he paced about impatiently until a rather flustered man appeared. He introduced himself as "Jim" and apologised for being late, explaining that he was new to the escort team.

"It's a fantastic job, "Jim enthused, "I'm out and about all day and not cooped up in an office. I get to meet all sorts of people, lots of them. I'm taking you to the Earthly Team, is that right?"

"Yes, but I'd like to take a diversion and not go there just yet. Is that possible? Do you have the time?"

"I certainly do," said Jim, "and I need some practice; people can get very unpleasant if they think I'm not taking them by the best routes."

"Good, it'll suit us both," said Andy.

As they walked, Jim pointed out various departments; I.T., Journalism, Bread & Cakes, etc. Andy was gleeful when Jim produced his torch.

"Do you use the torch much?" he asked.

"All the time, couldn't manage without it. Mind you, if you don't programme it correctly it's no use at all. The system looks complicated but it isn't. The weekly code change is posted on our screens every morning. You have to be up early to catch it because it's only on -screen for thirty minutes or so. The departments are numbered in alphabetical order. You enter the number of the department you're leaving and the number of your destination, and add the weekly code and, hey presto, the torch will start to vibrate. When you're going the right way the torch shines with a bright, white, light. If you go wrong the light dims to a sort of grey. It's difficult to use at first because the difference in the torch's beam is not always obvious. I'll demonstrate for you," said Jim.

"Why hasn't it been obvious that a torch is being used?"

"Simple! Some clever dicks can navigate without the torches; others like you to think that they can, so they hide their torches up their sleeves."

Andy was so delighted at getting the information he needed, and so pleased that he hadn't been "thick" in failing to understand the codes, that he hugged his new friend. Jim allowed him to practise with the torch and he soon mastered the light changes. All he needed now was to discover where Peter kept the torch, and to be up early on the days when he needed the code. He was able to relax and enjoy the remainder of his stroll back to the Earthly Team building. His interview with Barrie had become a fading memory. By the time Andy and Jim arrived back, they'd become firm friends and parted in the hope of meeting again. Watching Jim walk away triggered warm memories of other friendships, but Andy pushed these aside for the time being to concentrate on finding the all important torch. He needed to keep an eye on Peter, so he didn't want to go to his room, neither did he want to be distracted by conversation, so he sat at his desk. He was instantly joined by Jeff, who wanted to know the details of his meeting with Barrie. Andy tried to discourage him by setting to work on a few trivial *requests* that had been lying on his desk for a few days. To Andy's surprise his ploy worked and Jeff retreated to his own corner, leaving Andy free to focus on his quest for the torch. Having endured several uneventful days during which most *requests* found their way into the waste bin, Andy finally had some luck. It was quiet in the office, too early for Jeremy to be up and about. Jeff was nowhere to be seen, and Peter and Sarah were busy at their desks, when Peter's green light began to flash .Responding to the summons, Peter quickly released the torch from beneath his desk and left. When he returned an hour or so later he put the torch back in the same place. Andy even went without meals in order to watch Peter all day, making sure he didn't change the torch's whereabouts.

Much later, when the majority of his colleagues were in their respective rooms and Jeremy was lost in his newspaper. Andy took his chance. After an anxious few moments fumbling with the torch, he managed to pull it free. He entered the correct settings and left the building without troubling with the Destination Book. "Why should I have to log my movements? After all," he reasoned, "I'm a free man, not a prisoner."

Chapter 18

Andy followed the bright light and was elated by how easy it all was. It took a little longer than he'd expected to reach the Fashion Department, but he thought this might be to his advantage. At the end of their working day, the team might be more relaxed and welcoming.

With his confidence growing, Andy decided to knock politely rather than barge in as he'd done before. He waited to be invited to enter. When a stranger opened the door he was a little unsure of himself, but he quickly recovered when the man was friendly and hospitable. He introduced himself as Harold, and didn't question Andy's request to see Alicia for fashion advice.

"Alicia, my dear, this young man has come to see you; did you say your name was Sandy?"

"It's Andy," Alicia said, smiling.

For a while the three of them sat chatting but, after a polite interlude, Alicia coaxed Harold into cutting a pattern for a new range of children's clothes. With Harold safely out of the way in the cutting room, Alicia turned to Andy.

"What can I do for you, Andy?"

"Nothing, I needed to see you to discuss something rather private. Is there any chance we could go to your room?"

"You know having guests in our rooms is viewed with disapproval. The philosophy of the Holding Station is to create cohesion through openness and equal access for all within our different stations. Balance is achieved by insisting on the privacy of our individual accommodation."

"Perhaps, on this one occasion, "Andy pleaded, "you could make an exception. I need the freedom to speak openly and I couldn't do that if anyone were to join us. Besides, it's been such a challenge getting here that I could use the opportunity to unwind."

"Of course, but just this once, you understand?"

Away from prying eyes in Alicia's room, Andy lost no time in pinning her against the wall. Thrusting his body firmly against hers, he kissed her face, neck, hands, and fingers passionately. The intensity of their desire coursed hotly through their bodies. It had been so long since Andy had enjoyed any sexual contact that he was unable and unwilling to restrain himself. His fervour was matched by Alicia's as they undressed each other with the swiftness and purpose of a hawk swooping on its prey. Intuitively they were aware their sexual appetites were well matched. Their intimacy was not that of a fledgling couple, they possessed the maturity and expertise to satisfy each other and, in this, they laid the foundation for future encounters.

They barely spoke before parting, except for expressing their happiness and to plan their next meeting. Andy said he would telephone as soon as he had the opportunity and, of course, the torch. He would allow the telephone to ring twice before replacing the receiver. Alicia would then return the call, letting the phone ring once. The arrangement would keep colleagues at bay and prevent them from trying to dissuade them from continuing with their relationship.

Andy's return journey was relaxed and pleasant, and he was able to negotiate the path with confidence. His unaccustomed contentment had several sources. He had enjoyed scintillating sex with Alicia, he'd mastered the use of the torch, he was free to move around, John was not a threat, and Harold was good company. Andy suddenly realised he was very hungry. He'd had an exciting day and had gone without food altogether. He planned to have an extravagant supper as a pleasant finale to his successful escapade. Jeremy was still up and about when Andy returned. His attempt to ease the obvious tension failed when Jeremy refused the coffee he was offered and bade Andy a rather unfriendly "good night". Jeremy's frostiness didn't upset Andy's mood. He returned the torch to its place under Peter's desk and retired to enjoy his sumptuous meal and a good night's sleep.

Chapter 19

The next evening Andy and Jeremy were relaxing in the lounge. Jeremy was dressed as usual and, for the first time, Andy thought he was quite a handsome man, "in an old kind of way."

"How are you?" asked Jeremy.

"Fine."

"I was thinking about your grandparents last night; I suppose they're sad you're no longer with them."

"What makes you think that?"

"People are usually saddened by the death of a young person."

"Shouldn't think they were; they didn't make much time for me while I was on earth."

Jeremy made clear just how unfortunate they thought Vanessa's choice of husband had been. It was about a year after her marriage that Frederick and Jean deduced from snippets of information that their precious daughter was living in a dangerous relationship. Talking about parents unsettled Andy at the best of times, but today it was truer than usual. The cause, however, was not his parents' unhappy marriage but the intrusion into his delicious thoughts about Alicia. In a bid to recapture the mood, he retreated to his desk and stared aimlessly at the screen.

It was Peter's harsh voice that shocked him back to reality.

"Did you go out last night?" Peter demanded.

"Certainly not! I was here all night," Andy lied.

"I have a *request* I want you to deal with. It's urgent and quite tricky, so you'll have to have your wits about you. I don't want any guesswork on this one; if you need help, ask for it. If I'm not available, speak to Jeff."

Briefly, Andy contemplated challenging the decision to pass this urgent *request* to him on the grounds that he'd not been consulted. However, he decided against it as he didn't want to create more diffi-culties for himself. He was already wondering who'd told Peter about his outing the night before. He knew Peter's enquiry wasn't merely random. The only person, apparently, who could have reported him was Jeremy. Although Jeremy had been annoyed with him, Andy rejected the notion of him being the culprit because Jeremy would view reporting his unauthorised absence as disloyalty to Frederick. Anyway, that would have to wait until later. Right now he had to deal with the urgent request. His performance would be scrutinised, he'd be unable to escape to his room, and he would have to succeed in order to acquire some kudos to help him to maintain the progress he'd made with Alicia.

Request: immediate medical intervention required for a man of advanced years.

Peter's direction was somewhat confusing; surely the skilled med-ical service could weave their magic and make short work of this emergency? He wondered if Peter was testing him, especially when he recommended consulting Jeff who, with the best will in the world, was not the sharpest knife in the drawer. Putting Alicia out of his mind, he turned to his screen and saw a strangely familiar scene. The post war semi-detached house with its net curtains, neat lawns, and well cared for garden was protected by a tall, brick wall and electroni-cally controlled, iron, gates, both of which were relatively recent addi-tions. Inside the house there were plenty of book-cases holding an impressive collection of books. The house was a little old-fashioned, but comfortable and well designed. Andy wondered why it seemed slightly familiar. Finally, he recognised his grandparents' home. In the largest bedroom he could see his grandfather, struck down by illness, being watched over by his wife.

"However will she live without him?" Andy asked himself. He needed help quickly and Peter and Jeremy weren't around. Remembering Peter's advice, he looked for Jeff, who was happy to help. "The same thing happened to me a few months ago with my uncle" he said, and Andy realised why Peter had told him to consult Jeff.

Andy and Jeff watched events unfolding. Jean had gone to another room to take a telephone call from Vanessa.

"Surely it isn't up to Stuart if you visit. Besides, even he could manage a party without you being there."

"Leave it with me, mum, and I'll get back to you."

Jean sat motionless, staring into space, until Vanessa rang back to say she was travelling up to Leeds immediately, and that Stuart had been in touch with an eminent doctor friend, who would be with her very soon. "of course you were right; I should be with you and dad. It's why Stuart's insisted that I leave at once and why he's offered to cover the costs of the journey and the doctor's expenses."

The doctor arrived soon afterwards and set to work at once. He said Frederick had suffered a slight stroke and that Jean's prompt action had prevented more serious damage. Jean was hugely relieved when he prescribed aspirin and said Frederick would be "right as rain" the next day. Jeff advised Andy to speak to Phil Jones on the Medical Team, who concurred with the doctor. Watching from his desk, Jeff reported "successful conclusion; you can get off to bed now" in the hope that Andy wouldn't hear his father talking to his friend, the doctor, who was reassuring him that Vanessa was staying in Leeds. This meant Stuart could take another woman to the party.

Frederick's poor health weighed heavily on Andy, and it caused some reassessment of his father. Had he been wrong to judge his father so harshly when he'd done so much to help Frederick and had unselfishly encouraged his wife to be with her parents? Seeing his grandparents' home had triggered some pleasant memories which didn't put his new situation in a good light. The sameness of his existence was disheartening. There were no nights; it was never hot or cold, never humid. He remembered windy, wet days when litter and leaves intermingled and swirled around his feet. He recalled lying beside a river, gazing at the sky, making pictures from the clouds. The clouds on the Holding Station only confused him.

Chapter 20

Most of the time Andy worked in close proximity to his colleagues, so it was a relief when they decided against giving him any new *requests* for the time being. He appreciated their kind intentions but, at the same time, he was irritated by them; he felt the darkness drawing across him again. After a few listless days, Andy's energy began to return. He hadn't entirely wasted the past few days; he'd discovered Peter's new hiding place for the torch, and he was ready and eager to spend more time with Alicia. Everything went smoothly. He took the torch and telephoned Alicia, using their prearranged code. He slipped out without signing the book and was startled when Peggy's voice boomed "Where are you off to?" She'd been smoking by doorway and exhaled an enormous cloud of smoke.

"An errand for Peter," Andy said the first thing that occurred to him.

"Hope you've signed out?"

"Yes."

He knew his latest lie could be easily detected but he calculated that the goodwill currently being extended to him would protect him from serious repercussions.

To Andy's delight, Alicia greeted him, looking as though she was anticipating a sexually intimate afternoon. She'd swapped her uniform for a revealing red dress and a pair of black, high-heeled, shoes. She also wore some heavy pieces of jewellery including a necklace that nestled between her breasts. Arm in arm, gazing into one another's eyes, they walked silently to Alicia's private room. Their love-making even surpassed their anticipation. They clung to each other with the desperation of desire. When, occasionally, they spoke, their words had little meaning or purpose. Each was completely besotted and content with the other and they were reluctant to bring their pleasures to an end. However, they both knew it was unwise for Andy to be away for too long. As Andy reached his own building he was struck once more by the starkness of the place. Peggy's cigarette butts were the only evidence of habitation.

"He must be up. I heard him blowing his nose at least three hours ago," Sarah was saying to someone.

There you are!" cried Peter, "your green light has been flashing for ages."

"Really....do you think I need to get over to Barrie's office?" Andy asked them.

"Well, that's the general idea," Peter snapped.

"You should get a move on, old chap," Jeremy advised him.

Andy was delighted to find that his escort was his friend, Jim. They chatted on their way to Barrie's office, and Andy told Jim about his visit to Alicia. He didn't think to ask Jim about the reason for Barrie's summons, and he gave it no special consideration. Consequently, he was taken off guard when Barrie was hostile and didn't even offer him coffee.

"You've been out without permission," she accused him.

"Yes. I was out," said Andy, "I had to get some advice from Alicia, you know, from the Fashion Department."

"I'm fully aware of where Alicia works."

"Any chance of a coffee?"

"I'm really not sure you understand the seriousness of your situation," said Barrie ignoring him. "You haven't settled into your team and their routines, and you haven't made appropriate use of the expert support available to you. I now have a challenge for you and I expect you to act responsibly. Jim will explain it all to you on your way back. Goodbye!" Barrie left the room without a word, leaving Andy confused and angry. Since their first meeting he'd taken it for granted that Barrie was fond of him, so he was crushed by her display of hostility. He'd already been concerned about how his meetings with Alicia had come to Barrie's attention, but now he had to worry about her criticism of his work performance as well. He was shaken and made sure he listened intently to what Jim had to say.

Jim's manager had persuaded him to help with Andy. His record of helpfulness and getting results made him a good choice. Barrie had gone out on a limb when she assigned Andy to the Earthly Team and, even with Gabriel's help, was finding it difficult to cope with his defiance. She needed outside help so that the situation could remain hidden from the Influencing Team, and Jim seemed to fit the bill. Barrie had seen Jim before her meeting with Andy. She said he appeared to have misunderstood his remit; she wanted him to give

Andy "direction" not "protection."

Jim was shaken over his error and it left him in the unenviable position of having to withdraw his friendliness. Andy was disappointed that Jim's manner had changed; he was now altogether more serious and stern. Jim explained that a new worker, Jenny, had been assigned to Andy's team and that he'd been chosen to be her mentor. Andy's heart sank.

Chapter 21

"It's a bloody woman." thought Jenny. When the old, grey-haired stranger had said she was going to meet Barrie, she'd assumed she was meeting a man. Hitching her skirt up and undoing an extra button on her blouse wasn't going to help her to achieve her goal of bypassing the lower levels and moving straight to Cloud Nine, or Nirvana, or wherever the most desirable places were. Jenny had been ambitious and, in her mid-twenties she regarded herself as a high-flyer. She'd certainly flown pretty high when the car had struck and killed her. She'd expected her career achievements to give her a head start, but she was quite mistaken, which added insult to fatal injury.

"Hello," Barrie greeted her, "I'll try to keep this as informal as possible. Would you like some coffee?"

Jenny was surprised to find something so "earthly" was available and wondered how they'd managed it. Sensing her surprise and curiosity, Barrie explained that some of the younger element had so badly missed the availability of a decent cup of coffee, that they had lobbied, successfully, for a Starbucks She admitted, however, that she'd drawn the line at their request for Pierre Marcolini chocolate.

"Dear me, this woman's quick," thought Jenny, "I hope she didn't pick up on my disappointment that she wasn't a man."

"I believe you were a nurse," said Barrie.

"Sister, actually. The youngest in my hospital."

"I've decided that you will be working with the Earthly Team. It's not especially busy, but the work can be complicated and require sensitivity."

"Actually, I wanted the Fashion Department."

"I'm afraid they don't have a vacancy," Barrie told her.

"Oh, why did I go for that packet of fags? Jenny thought ruefully.

If she'd stayed at home, she'd be alive today. Wasn't it bad enough that her arrival had been so low key? Now she was obliged to accept that she'd have to work on the Earthly Team. Sorting out the personal problems of earthly folk was not an attractive option to Jenny. Before her accident she'd decided to leave nursing, having lost interest in her career and becoming bored with listening to the moans and groans of the sick. On top of everything else it seemed she would have to wear an unflattering uniform. From the frumpish cream blouse to the flat, black, shoes, the outfit did nothing for Jenny.

"Did you meet the team on the way in?" asked Barrie.

"Yes." Jenny lowered her tone in an attempt to hide her feelings. In fairness, the Team had tried to reassure her that she'd soon "Settle". However, she had no intention of settling. She intended to obtain advancement by impressing Barrie with her varied talents. Exhausted by all her meetings, Barrie concluded Jenny's interview and pressed the green button to summon Jeff. She told him to escort Jenny to the Earthly Team and to wait with her until Andy arrived to take over. A few minutes later, Gabriel, Barrie's oldest and most trusted friend, arrived. They made themselves comfortable, kicked off their shoes, and sipped gin and tonics. They agreed the day had been amusing, and pondered Jenny's and Andy's chances of success. They decided there was too much uncertainty to be able to calculate the odds.

Chapter 22

Gabriel had been around the Holding Station for millennia prior to Barrie's arrival there but, unlike Jenny, he was pleased to discover she was a woman and the pair quickly formed a warm, lasting, friendship. Barrie was in her sixties when she checked in following a prolonged, painful, illness. She welcomed the release from pain, but it was difficult for her to leave her husband, children, and grandchildren. She greatly loved and admired her husband, Leonard, which made it possible for her to cope with his interest in young men. He was always discreet and scrupulously sexually responsible. When Barrie died her children grieved for her, but their grief turned to anger when Leonard invited a handsome young man into the marital home. During intimate times before her death, Barrie admitted to Leonard that she had always been aware of his young men and made him promise to follow his desires after she'd gone. Once established in the Influencing Team, she selected the most honest and reliable man for her beloved Leonard, and never sought to intrude into his life again.

Chapter 23

"How did you get along with Barrie?" Andy asked. Jenny was adamant that her meeting had gone well, managing to conceal her indignation at being assigned to such a lowly position. Andy found her attitude irritating and he was delighted when the eruption of molten rock startled her. He did nothing to reassure her, merely wandering off and leaving her alone. Jenny wasn't concerned by Andy's lack of attention, she was more curious about the eruption and the furore it caused. From what Jenny could make out there were several of the teams personnel studying papers that appeared to have come from the fax machine. She was still perplexed by her new situation where the familiar frequently coexisted with the bizarre, where some things had scarcely changed whilst others were entirely new and different. Her equanimity wasn't helped by Andy's roving eye resting on her cleavage. She made an attempt to adjust her clothes while Andy happily watched her embarrassment. He planted two cups of coffee on the desk and pointed at the sugar, which was solid from constant use.

"Yes...two." Jenny said.

"I've been tasked with mentoring you, "said Andy," and tomorrow I'll begin your training with a lesson on the wondrous workings of the fax machine."

Sarah broke Andy's flow when she entered their conversation

"I think you two have already met," Andy said.

"Yes, a little earlier. If you need help and Andy's not about, please don't hesitate to call on me. After all, he's rarely where he's supposed to be. By the way, Peggy will have a cigarette if you need one, but be careful, separating Peggy from a cigarette can be difficult even for the most able amongst us."

"Thank goodness she's gone; nice, but a bit fussy," said Andy as Sarah moved away. Jenny wasn't listening. She was wondering how Sarah knew she was a smoker; she hadn't had one since her arrival. Now, however, Sarah's mention of them had brought back her craving.

Andy told Jenny how to find her private room and explained the workings of the food machine. "It looks more complicated than it is. Just press the button opposite your chosen meal and it'll arrive through the tube at the bottom within the hour. Look, Honey," he continued," I'm going to call it a day. I've got a meeting later and, quite frankly, I'm exhausted. By the way, if you happen to bump into the others, just tell them you needed a rest, cheers," said Andy, and, making his exit with a dismissive wave, he was gone, leaving Jenny to fend for herself.

She walked the full length of the partition between the office area and lounge on the one hand, and the private accommodation on the other, before finding her own room at the far end. Being alone in the eerie silence made her new surroundings seem even more alien. She sat on the bed, her small, slender, body too light to make any impression on the mattress. The full length mirror on the opposite wall revealed the rich, auburn, hair framing her face and her eyes, presently devoid of emotion. She was vaguely interested in the replicas of some of her favourite bits and pieces, all in pristine condition. Her precious gold coloured frame was prominently displayed. It held a photograph of her mother and brothers. She stared so longingly at their picture that she hardly registered the empty frame alongside it.

Suddenly aware of being hungry, Jenny examined the cumbersome food machine that occupied one whole side of the room. As she'd been told, the variety of meals available was impressive; some were entirely familiar, but others were completely unknown to her and she couldn't even guess at what they were She wanted something homely, and selected sausage and mash with a cup of tea. Jenny undressed and put on the pyjamas provided for her. Sleep didn't come easily and she tossed and turned, restlessly, for hours. She must have dropped off for a minute or two, however, she was awoken by thumping on her door.

It was Andy. As soon as he'd left Jenny on her own he'd realised it had been a mistake. If his ill-considered departure was discovered there could be unfortunate repercussions. He knew he'd have to sort things out with Jenny; he couldn't afford to have her complaining about him to someone else. He realised that although Jenny seemed to be reserved, she was certainly no push over. He hadn't been able to deal with the situation earlier because he'd been with Alicia but now, satisfied and confident, he felt able to handle his protégée. He was pleased to find her in a flatter, less ebullient, mood. He left after telling her he'd return shortly and suggesting that she should make herself pretty in the meantime. He was pleased with himself and left Jenny's room with a broad smile on his face. He'd miscalculated. His parting remark had changed Jenny's apathy into anger. She was certainly not going to wait around for Andy's return and set off to find him. Andy was chatting with Sarah and Jeff near the coffee machine and Jenny was about to challenge his mentoring credentials when she was interrupted by an upsurge of the molten rock. "Damn," said Sarah, "It's another *request* from Alex Jones wanting a date with Madonna. Those bloody Americans and their preoccupation with Positive Thinking! It's grown and grown, and generated far too much additional work. This job isn't what it was. We used to have proper *requests* from desperate people wanting us to rescue them from poverty and despair. I think I'll ask for a transfer to the African Team - they have real problems."

Convinced that he could manoeuvre his way through any difficulty, and seeking to gain the advantage, Andy steered Jenny towards his desk and, sitting down with his feet on the desk, suggested that she get them both a drink. His suggestion was really an instruction. Back on Earth, Jenny would have managed such arrogance, but not here. Andy had her in the palm of his hand and she could do nothing about it. She was on her way back with the coffees when Sarah called for help. "Crap"" said Andy. He'd been aware the molten rock was rumbling but had ignored it because he was enjoying himself watching Jenny having to dance to his tune. Sarah's call for help forced him to stop his game and go to the aid of his colleague.

Chapter 24

Jenny sat, hunched, on her bed, her chin resting on her knees and her arms wrapped around her legs as if she were holding herself together. She felt abandoned, lost, and uncomfortable. Her body was trembling and her usual composure had deserted her. Gazing out of her window she saw the Earth and watched as snowflakes descended on Manchester. The scene evoked vivid childhood memories which she thought had been buried forever. Their re-emergence precipitated a flood of unstoppable tears.

Just before Jenny's eighth birthday a man had knocked on her front door. She was unaware until later that the man, Jonathan, would become an important part of her life. He was a social worker and she would like him and loathe him, but never completely trust him. Her mother, Kaye, dashed downstairs to answer the door before her three year old son, Sean, could open it. From a mixture of boredom and excitement, Sean's curiosity was aroused and he wanted to know who was calling, especially as callers were such a rarity. Besides, opening the door gave him an opportunity to demonstrate how "grown up" he was by dragging the stool across the hallway and climbing onto it so that he could reach the door handle.

He was too young to understand the house rules for getting rid of unwanted callers which denied entry to anybody who didn't use the "safe signal" of three deliberate raps followed by two, in rapid succession. Kaye was just too late to stop Sean opening the door. Besides, with the commotion in the hall it was obvious that someone was at home. As she reached the bottom stair her worst fears were realised when she saw Ronnie, her husband, standing in the living room, hidden from the caller's view, his face contorted with rage. Kaye scooped Sean into her arms before kicking the stool aside to open the front door. She recognised the man blocking out most of the daylight with his large frame as Jonathan, one of the new breed of social workers working alongside teaching staff for a couple of days each week. "Hello, Kaye, "Jonathan said, "Mrs. Millwood has asked me to call. She's concerned about Jenny's and Craig's poor school attendance; they've been absent rather a lot lately."

Jonathan had met Kaye on a couple of occasions when he tried to help her to improve the children's school attendance, but he'd had little success. Late arrival at nursery didn't matter much in Sean's case. Whenever Kaye turned up, Sean ran in and enthusiastically joined which ever children he thought were having the most fun. He could become troubled if he missed the early morning snack, but nudging his favourite teacher sorted things out and he calmed down. It was very different for Jenny and Craig who were deeply embarrassed by their late arrivals. They would try to slip quietly into class. This was easier when the other children were sitting on rugs in front of the teacher rather than at their tables. It wasn't unusual for Mrs. Millwood to give them some milk and toast before taking them into their class. Mrs. Millwood thought the children's lack of alertness, poor presentation, and unresponsiveness proved that all was not well in the Clark household.

Kaye hesitated. Should she keep Jonathan on the doorstep, drawing the attention of her neighbours, or should she risk Ronnie's anger by inviting him inside? Jonathan took the matter out of her hands by insisting they conduct their business in private. Kaye directed Jonathan to the kitchen, still holding Sean in her arms. Jenny and Craig walked purposefully between the adults as though forming a human barrier between them. Jonathan, glancing around him, noticed there was a man in the house. He took him to be Kaye's husband and the children's father. He was slumped in an armchair, engrossed in a television programme, and he chose not to acknowledge Jonathan's greeting.

The kitchen was sparsely furnished; there were a couple of cupboards on the wall, a free standing gas cooker, and a table with four chairs. The floor was covered in blue lino which was faded and cracked. The walls were dirty and there was a smell of grease. Sensitively, and in ways the children wouldn't understand, Jonathan broached the subject of their welfare. Apart from their poor attendance, they appeared to be underweight, and some of their vaccinations were outstanding. "Everything's fine, "Kaye protested, "can't see what all the fuss is about. I had a few difficulties over the weekend that's all. I just couldn't get the uniforms dry in time - the radiators don't work properly and I couldn't afford the launderette. I'll sort it out and send them later." "Good, I'll be on my way then," Jonathan said, relieved that Kaye had cooperated, albeit with a slight edge of hostility.

Now he'd be able to "get the ball rolling" by drawing up a support plan with Kaye. He realised she was an intelligent and capable woman being dragged down by extremely unfortunate circumstances. She seemed embarrassed whenever they ran into each other; she would look away and hurry off. Jonathan thought he might be able to gain Ronnie's cooperation in time but, for now, he knew Ronnie would resist any plan involving his family. Kaye was still in the kitchen when Jonathan closed the door behind him. He was well out of ear shot when Ronnie launched into a tirade of abuse aimed at his captive audience.

"I told you to get those bloody kids to school today, and who opened the door? I'm not having any shit calling from the social services to tell me what I should do with my kids." Having finished his rant, Ronnie returned to his armchair and resumed drinking the whisky which he had safely parked beside his chair and out of sight. He had been too drunk to notice the children weren't at school that morning, and blissfully unaware that Kaye had replenished his whisky the evening before when she'd noticed his supply was running low. She was not being generous. Far from it. It was necessary to avoid the unpleasantness that always resulted from Ronny's involuntary detoxification. The whisky had taken all her money and she'd been unable to visit he launderette.

Reluctantly, she told Jenny and Craig they wouldn't be going to school the following day. Craig was pleased. He wasn't fond of school, he found the work challenging and the other children were mean to him. He was small and his poor complexion made him look sickly. On top of this his red hair and poor clothing made him a butt for unkind jibes. He never told his mother about his school misery because he didn't want to worry her. He knew the other children were aware that he had no one to stick up for him. He felt vulnerable and isolated and generally had to play alone.

Jenny had a very different view of school. For her, school was a refuge, away from the tensions which had become a natural part of her home life. She was bored when she was at home because she had to stay indoors in case she was spotted by Truancy Enforcement Officers. Sometimes Jenny thought her mother deliberately created situations to keep her away from school, so she had been secretly cheered when Jonathan had called that morning.

Jenny was bright and fully able to outwit her peers as she successfully manoeuvred her way around the school yard politics. She transferred the skills she'd learned when assessing and coping with her father's moods to dealing with her peers at school. With the atmosphere seemingly calm again, Kaye led her children through the living room and upstairs. Ronnie was once more engrossed in the television. He enjoyed joining in and addressing his own opinions to the television screen; it pleased him to remain unchallenged in this. Kaye tried to see the room through the eyes of a stranger and was dismayed. There was no natural light because Ronnie insisted on keeping the curtains permanently closed. He claimed that they reduced the noise from the street but, in truth, he liked the feeling of being cut off and separate. Years of smoking, eating, and drinking alcohol, had produced odours that now permeated everything in the room, mainly the odd assortment of second hand furniture that Kaye had managed to collect over the years. The once vivid yellow curtains were now brown, tarnished in much the same way as Ronnie's body. This room was Ronnie's sanctuary, and no one was allowed in without his permission. Kaye and the children were only allowed to pass through on their way to other parts of the house. Ronnie seldom left his room except to use the toilet or to get washed, and the latter was getting less and less frequent.

Since the birth of their youngest child, Kaye had slept alone as Ronnie preferred to remain downstairs. Recently, Kaye had managed to buy a cheap television from a charity shop, but the reception was poor as she only had an indoor aerial. By contrast, Ronnie had a large, multi-channel set attached to an outdoor aerial. Kaye did not challenge this because it kept her husband quiet whilst she and the children snuggled together in her bed watching the early evening programmes.

It was several hours after Jonathan's departure that Craig complained of being hungry. Being without food or money, Kaye coaxed Jenny into going to the local grocery shop where she could buy, on tick, the basic ingredients for a decent meal. Although she hated her task, Jenny was delighted by the prospect of a trip to Jackie's general store. The shop was small compared to the larger supermarkets, but some nook or cranny would hold the most unlikely surprises.

Had Jenny considered it, she would not have believed that her mother and Jackie were the same age, for the two could not have been more different. Jenny's view of her mother was that she was drab and unattractive with a poor complexion, shabby clothing, and always looking weary. In contrast, Jackie was alert and immaculately presented. She went regularly to the hairdresser and manicurist and shopped for fashionable clothes whenever she could grab the opportunity. Kaye had no inkling of her daughter's views, being so burdened by the unexpected twists and turns in her life. Jenny often felt twinges of guilt when, out of shame, she discouraged her mother from attending school events; sometimes she didn't even tell her about them. Jackie didn't hesitate to give Jenny the items she asked for as Kaye always paid her debts as soon as she was able. Jenny lingered in Jackie's company for as long as she could, before having to leave, certain that Jackie would have added some treats for each child as usual, having been saddened by the hopeless expression on Jenny's face and a desire to brighten the children's day. Over a period of time Jackie had often seen bruising on Kaye's face and neck and wondered why she tolerated such an abusive relationship. She didn't understand how every blow destroyed a little more of Kaye's self-esteem and, with it, her hope.

Over the next few months Kaye met with Jonathan on a couple of occasions. The children's time keeping improved with the help of some transport arrangements and the occasional financial support. Kaye's gradual acceptance of Jonathan's help was encouraging and he sometimes sensed she was almost about to confide in him when she suddenly back peddled once more.

Chapter 25

It was the evening before the arrival of the benefit payment when the eruption began. Kaye was acutely aware of the danger she and the children were in as a consequence of her having been unable to replenish Ronnie's whisky. Even so, the level of his rage took her by surprise. As usual, Kaye and the children were hugged together watching television when, without warning, Ronnie flung open the bedroom door raving that he needed whisky and shouting that he wouldn't have any interfering bastards from social services barging into his house telling him what to do with his kids. Cowering in fear, Kaye sidled past her husband and went into the bathroom, hoping that she was safe to leave her children in the bedroom.

She didn't have time to lock the door before Ronnie attacked her, raining heavy blows on her face and body. "Who does he think he is? That worm, coming into my house and telling me to get my children to school, and you, haven't you got the sense to get them there?" he demanded. Kaye, cornered in the bathroom, couldn't escape and Ronnie's blows continued to rain down. She tried to muffle her cries but they still reached the children's ears. Horrified, Sean hid beneath the bedclothes hoping the assault would soon come to an end and that Kaye would return to comfort him. Craig couldn't get beyond the bedroom door. Jenny hurled herself between her parents, but Ronnie's fist caught her on the cheek and she fell against the bathroom sink. "Now look what you've made me do, you stupid bitch!" Ronnie roared. Kaye was full of hate towards her husband as she watched him walk away downstairs without offering any comfort or help to his daughter. She cleaned Jenny's grazed face and covered the injury with the remains from a tube of antiseptic cream. Eventually, Kaye and the three children slept, their arms still around one another.

Their sleep was uneasy and interrupted by sobs. In spite of her pain, Kaye managed to get her children to school on time. Her bruises did not yet show, so there was little evidence of the previous night's events. It was painful for her to stand up straight, but she was able to bear it long enough to see the children into school.

Earlier she'd primed the children to give the same version of events if they were pressed for information, and to say nothing otherwise. She hoped the explanation that Jenny had fallen over and cut her face on the corner of a wall would satisfy any curious professionals and others who might question the children during the day. Nervously, Kaye took Sean into his nursery before watching Craig dragging his bag and his feet reluctantly into the infants' playground while Jenny raced into the juniors' yard to join her friends and play.

It was a little before lunch when Mrs. Millwood called Jenny out of her classroom and took her along to her room. As Mrs. Millwood discreetly closed her door Jenny overheard Jonathan saying that Kaye would be joining them shortly. This helped to quell Jenny's fear that her mother's absence meant she was seriously hurt, or worse, dead. The formality of the occasion persuaded Jenny that something was seriously wrong. "Jenny," Jonathan said, "Mrs. Millwood has kindly agreed to us waiting in her room until your mother arrives. Because I thought you might be hungry I've brought an assortment of biscuits and a drink. Just help yourself to anything on the coffee table."

Jenny made a protective, defensive, barrier by crossing her arms tightly across her stomach before gingerly sitting next to Jonathan and faithfully repeating the prepared account of how she injured her forehead. She was reaching for the largest biscuit when Mrs. Millwood entered the room closely followed by Kaye. Once a few awkward pleasantries had been exchanged, Mrs. Millwood suggested that Jenny might like to join her friends for lunch and, with an affectionate smile, prompted her to take some biscuits with her.

The distress was audible in Jonathan's voice as he explained to Kaye why his colleague had called to the house insisting that she attend this meeting. He told her he'd arranged for Jenny to be examined by a paediatrician. He needed to know whether her account of her injury was acceptable as it hadn't tallied with Craig's. Craig had told his teacher "it happened when Daddy was shouting at mummy." Kaye knew it was pointless to withhold her permission as it would merely force Jonathan to obtain a court order allowing the examination to take place. Inevitably, the children's fate was sealed when the paediatrician reported that the injury had been caused by an adult's fist.

Kaye returned home by herself, and her children moved in with Auntie Joan. Kaye was devastated by her loss, but convinced that all would be well and the children returned, once Ronnie saw the consequences of his destructive behaviour.

"It's not possible for your mum to come with you to Auntie Joan's, " Jonathan told the children, " but you will see her at the Family Centre after school tomorrow." Sean had no idea what Jonathan meant by going to "stay with Auntie Joan." He didn't have an auntie, let alone one called Joan. For Jenny and Craig it was a shattering blow not to be going home with their mother, and it was hard to grasp the significance of him saying they were "not safe" with their father.

Jenny let out a piercing scream that echoed round the clinic; her panic was caused by Ronnie's repeated warnings, and threats, that any defiance would result in a social worker taking them away and locking them up somewhere where they would get no food. To the children, not being able to go home meant they must have been very naughty. Kaye did her best to comfort and reassure them, but they were inconsolable. Eventually, she promised to see them every day and to "get the best solicitor" to help her bring them home.

Chapter 26

It was late evening when Jonathan parked in front of Joan's house. He'd known her for a long time and had confidence in her ability to console and soothe children. The three youngsters had cried incessantly since being waved off by their distraught mother. Jonathan had driven the twenty odd miles in silence. He could think of nothing worthwhile to say, nothing he believed would comfort the children and reduce their distress. They had been torn away from everything familiar to them, and the separation had been devastating. Moreover, tonight they would be unable to lie in bed with their mother, despite desperately needing the comfort she always gave them.

Joan had had plenty of experience in welcoming distressed, displaced children and knew that she had a vital ally in her trusty mongrel, Daisy. The three children sat in the back of the car stroking and cuddling Daisy, the flow of tears gradually subsiding as Joan told them about her and answered the unasked questions she knew they had in mind but were, for the time being, too timid to voice. With the children's agreement, everyone went into the house. Joan showed them around. Her house was very comfortable if a little old fashioned but, with little to compare it to, the children were mesmerised by its warmth, comfy chairs, and soft carpets. Sean was startled by Joan's invitation to sit down. "You mean we can sit in the living room?" he asked her. The children were comforted by the discovery that Sean and Craig would share a bedroom whilst Jenny had her own and, of course, the light would be left on.

Before leaving, Jonathan agreed with Joan that the children should stay off school for a few days as they needed to rest and to adjust to their new situation. Besides there would be a host of questions from their school friends and Joan would need time to help them prepare suitable answers. Jonathan said he'd advise Mrs. Millwood accordingly.

Joan encouraged the children to put a variety of foods on the table and allowed them to choose the ones they wanted. Encouraged by their hunger, and by Jenny, the boys tucked in, constantly checking that it was safe to continue. While the children were absorbed in their meal, Joan took the opportunity to ask about their likes and dislikes across a range of different areas. Jenny was less forthcoming than her brothers; her trust in adults began to diminish as her responsibility for shaping the direction of her own life and the lives of Craig and Sean increased. There were many times when a dig from Jenny would stop her brothers in mid sentence, although her interruption might later result in arguments between them. For now, however, Jenny was at the mercy of an endless flow of strangers who weaved in and out of her life with never-ending questions. Jenny knew her answers would influence their opinions and their plans for her.

Chapter 27

Jenny was always mindful of her father's description of Jonathan as a "worm". He thought of Jonathan as someone who slithered around underground, only popping up to meddle in other people's lives before going back when he'd caused maximum damage. Ronnie was critical of most people and this made it more difficult for Jenny and Craig to confide in other people or to trust them. Whenever Jenny plucked up the courage to ask Jonathan when she would be going home, he could only tell her that the final decision rested with the judge in court. Jenny wondered how this could be, when she and her brothers hadn't committed any crime. Jonathan did his best to explain Family Law and the court's responsibility for the children's safety and well-being, but this was almost impossibly difficult. In the end he always repeated that whatever she, "Craig and Sean wanted, would be heard in court."

Kaye was unable to tell her daughter anything concrete and reliable about her situation or future, so Jenny was left in constant limbo. It seemed completely unfair that she wasn't at home whilst the man responsible for her misery was still in the house. For most of a year she continued to live with Joan and saw her mother three or four times a week at the Family Centre. The Family Centre was chosen to ensure safety should Ronnie decide to visit his children. Of course, he never did, complaining "the arrangements were bloody stupid," and accusing Kaye of having created the situation and now doing nothing to make it better.

The time spent with Kaye was profoundly difficult for the children as they tried not to tell her about the exciting adventures they'd been having. Jenny took the lead as they navigated their way through their few hours together. Craig and Sean mopped up much of the time, excitedly persuading their mum to join in with their games. There was always the worry that anything they said or did might find its way back to Jonathan, but Jenny and Kaye talked privately in the toilets. The large, uninviting, room contained just one cubicle for adults, the remainder being toilets and sinks specifically designed for the under fives which gave the illusion of being in Alice's Wonderland. The Family Centre staff went to considerable lengths to provide an environment which would delight and enthral children. The walls were covered with favourite cartoon characters, and lots and lots of toys were available to play with and tumble around on. Later on, when Kaye and her children were together in a more or less empty room, the space felt eerie and inhospitable, and gave off a suggestion of wrong-doing. Kaye was often vague during these quieter moments, and Jenny was intent on protecting her mother by glossing over any difficulties when answering her questions about her new home and school. Jenny was comforted by Kaye's gentleness when she brushed her daughter's hair and told her how pretty she was, but these interludes never really eased her aching heart. As time went by, Jenny saw less and less of her mother and stopped asking about going home; it was apparent that this was never going to happen.

Chapter 28

"This just isn't fair on the children!" cried Jonathan.

He was furious. Not only would the children be separated, but they would also have to change schools. It was almost a year since Jonathan had taken the children to stay with Joan, and now it was time for permanent plans to be made. Much had occurred during the children's time with Joan, notably the impressive progress they'd made in all aspects of their life. Jonathan had failed, however, to persuade Kaye to leave Ronnie. While she remained with her husband the judge had ordered that the children could not go home.

Limited resources made the making of permanent plans extremely difficult. Jenny ended up moving to new foster carers, Mary and David Thompson. Craig and Sean moved together to live with Lucy and John. The children now lived further away from their schools and transport could not be funded, so they were obliged to leave behind well established friendships and teachers who had given all kinds of help, gentle affection, and praise.

Jonathan's manager agreed with him that changing schools would be detrimental, but there was little that could be done. Having so little control over his work left Jonathan angry and dispirited. Adding insult to injury, he was now required to explain the plans to the children, plans that didn't include their most ardent desire, a return home. Contemplating the day ahead weighed heavily on Jonathan as he silently ate his breakfast with his family around him. He was jogged out of his daydream by his four children goading and teasing each other. He compared their advantages over the children he worked with, wondering what the future held for Jenny and her brothers. If history was anything to go by it would probably be short on opportunity and freedom.

Joan was well practiced at preparing children for moving away from her care. Nevertheless, on the day of their move, sadness and anxiety prevailed as, once again, three tearful children were about to enter an unfamiliar world. As the moment approached for them to get into Jonathan's car, Joan gave each child a warm, tight, hug, and a bag of sweets containing her 'phone number. Jenny telephoned Joan on a couple of occasions during the first few weeks, but the calls soon dwindled. Joan never saw Craig or Sean again.

Chapter 29

Six months later, wearing two jumpers and a jacket because of the cold, Jenny meticulously followed the instructions given to her by Gwyneth and placed three, flat, stones in a straight line, three inches apart, under the sycamore tree at the end of the garden. Gwyneth had assured her friend that by following the instructions precisely a covering of snow would transform the stones and they would develop magical properties. Jenny felt a sense of urgency as spring was about to take over from winter, and snow was becoming more unlikely. Jenny believed whatever Granddad Johnson, her foster mother's father, told her, so she was disappointed by the absence of the white blanket he'd assured her would arrive "any time now." A little before midnight, three days after Granddad Johnson's prediction, Jenny was kneeling on her bed with Percy and Gareth, her foster parents' boys. They were peering skywards waiting for the snow to fall. Gradually the boys became too tired to stay awake and went off to their own beds to sleep.

Percy was not persuaded by Jenny's story. At nine he was a year younger than her and certain that there was not a grain of truth in the fable and, besides, he didn't much like Gwyneth. Five year old Gareth was desperate for the story to be true, but said nothing for fear of infuriating his brother who, when in a good mood, allowed him to play with his train set. What he really wanted was for the tale to be true and for Jenny to give him a wish - then he'd have his own train set.

Eventually, Jenny gave in as well and snuggled down under the fluffy duvet thinking how this house contrasted starkly with her own home. Tonight she was grateful for the comfort and warmth this one afforded her. Morning came swiftly and with it a rush of disappointment as Jenny saw the landscape was unchanged. In a flash she washed, dressed, and ran downstairs to have her breakfast. Mary was quite taken aback to find her most recent charge ready for school as she generally called her several times before she made an appearance, and then had to hurry her along with constant reminders about taking the things she needed for her day in school.

Mary didn't think there was any special significance in Jenny's behaviour, she was just vaguely pleased about it. Still eating her toast, Jenny ran out of the house. She bumped into David, almost knocking him over. "Hey! be careful," he shouted, but Jenny made no attempt to respond as she dashed off to Gwyneth's house. It was vital that she got a chance to quiz her during their walk to school as she couldn't be sure of getting another chance at playtimes. Crucially, the possibility of snow falling was diminishing, and Jenny needed to know if there was an alternative to snow that could weave the same magic. Breathless when she arrived at Gwyneth's house, Jenny was frustrated because her friend was not yet dressed and hadn't had her breakfast. Jenny contained her mounting frustration lest it spilled over and triggered an argument resulting in silence. After what seemed like an age, the pair began their walk to school.

"Gwyneth, I, er, wonder if there's another way for the stones to become magic," Jenny began.

"Don't know what you're talking about," replied her friend.

"The stones. Think, Gwyneth, think. A couple of weeks ago you told me that if I put three stones under a sycamore tree, three inches apart, and snow fell on them, they'd become magic stones," said Jenny.

"What are you talking about? Listen, did I tell you mum's taking me to Tenerife for my birthday. I'm chuffed. And she promised to buy me loads of clothes to take with me," said Gwyneth. Talk of clothes created a brief distraction as Jenny recalled a time, long ago, when she returned from a friend's birthday party with some nice clothes her friend's mother had given her. Jenny's delight quickly disappeared as she watched her father shred the clothes; "we don't need any bloody charity," he'd shouted, and he'd forbidden her friendship.

"Come on, try to remember. Oh, Gwyneth try, try, try, it's important," Jenny pleaded.

"OK, yes I do remember now; it will only work if it snows on the stones. Simply nothing else will work," said Gwyneth.

"But why not?"

"Because...oh, I don't know, just because! My uncle's friend told him that before the stones had any chance of becoming magic, snow had to fall on them." This blow to Jenny's hopes hit her hard. She knew she would have little chance of speaking to Gwyneth's uncle, let alone her uncle's friend. Jenny had no option but to accept the information she'd already been given - and to hope for snow. As the pair walked on, Gwyneth described the clothes she'd chosen, but Jenny paid no attention.

She was longing to be with her own mother, and for her to be buying her new clothes. Her longing was all consuming. Jenny rarely talked about her home life. Gwyneth knew Mary and David were not her "proper parents". Jenny referred to them as "mum and dad" at school but called them by their first names at home. She told Gwyneth it was "just easier." Gwyneth thought it was all rather strange, but gave the matter little further thought.

By the end of the school day, Jenny's teacher, Miss Davis, had been unable engage her in any way. Jenny was distracted by thoughts of the evening ahead. Jonathan, or "worm" as Jenny called him when she was in a bad mood, had set up a visit to see her brothers at their foster home, and he was very keen on maintaining the children's contact with each other. Today, however, Jenny didn't want to be away from the stones in case it snowed. She considered various strategies for avoiding the visit to see her brothers but, in the end, she went. Generally, she enjoyed spending time with Lucy and John but tonight was an exception because she badly wanted to be at home, keeping an eye on the three stones. She had no idea how long the stones would retain their magical properties, and she didn't know whether the magic worked if the snow failed to stick. For once, Lucy's attempts to conjure up a successful evening didn't work. Jenny's mood sank further and further with every passing minute. She endured the next few hours with her brothers and their "make shift" parents but the evening was dire and nothing could lift it. She was given her favourite foods, pizza and sponge cake covered in chocolate sauce, but didn't really appreciate them. Later, round the dining table, the conversation turned to discussing ideas for things to do when the weather improved. It was true that her relationship with Craig and Sean was gradually disintegrating because of different interests and lack of familiarity, but normally Jenny would have entered into these discussions with gusto, delighted at the prospect of new adventures and experiences. This evening, however, the discussions were just another interminable delay when what she wanted was to get home as quickly as possible. After dinner, while her brothers played games, she watched a DVD, especially bought for her by Lucy, but her lacklustre mood continued right up until David called to collect her at 8.30pm.

"Have a good time?" David asked her.

"Alright."

"I thought we might stop and play our special game before stopping to collect a takeaway," David said.

Jenny's heart sank. She always felt uncomfortable playing David's game and tonight there was the additional desire to get home as soon as possible in case it snowed. It was a colossal relief when Mary called to cancel the takeaway as Gareth was feeling unwell and she wanted David to return immediately.

Chapter 30

Jenny remained with Mary and David until leaving to take up a career in nursing. During the intervening years, she largely gave up on the "magic stones" as an escape to greater happiness and settled into her life with her foster parents. There were compensations to living in "care" such as regular meals, clean clothes, and holidays. The house was full of books which she was encouraged to read. They filled her lonely hours, and fed her imagination, but they did little to dispel the ache in her heart. On the rare occasions snow fell, Jenny checked the stones for magical properties. This wasn't out of conviction but from nostalgia for a time when her hope outweighed everything else. The last time snow fell, it came late one evening but Jenny waited until the middle of the night before creeping downstairs and slipping quietly into the garden. She knelt before the stones as she'd done so many years before. Picking up each one, she repeated the words she'd rehearsed so often, "please let me and my brothers go home to my mother and my father be gone."

There had been one time when Jenny had tried to extricate herself from her "captivity", when she couldn't face more years of living with people chosen for her by social workers. She hoped to move to a hostel specifically intended for young, homeless people some thirty miles away. Slipping a few belongings into her school bag she left home at the usual time and made her way to the bus station. When she went into the social services office the duty officer, Frances, was in the middle of her lunch. Although slightly irritated by the intrusion, she had no option but to see Jennifer and to record their conversation. Frances had been planning to deal with a mound of outstanding paperwork, but Jenny's request scuppered all that.

Before she could drive away in her old banger, Frances had to shift a pile of papers and bag and dispose of a pile of rubbish, just to let Jenny into the passenger seat. When they arrived at the hostel they were met by the manager, Pauline, who explained that Jenny was too young to be given accommodation there.

With a little coaxing, Jenny told Frances how she'd travelled the thirty miles or so by bus as she was miserable where she lived and wanted to leave and return to her own home or live independently. She admitted that she had a social worker and made no protest when Frances said she'd contact Jonathan; her usual boldness had been replaced by uncertainty. This was the first time Jenny had been on her own in unfamiliar territory and the experience wasn't as liberating as she'd supposed it would be. Having arranged to meet Jonathan in a couple of hours the pair filled in the time by heading for the park after picking up some food. During the journey, Jenny opened the window before lighting a cigarette, she flashed a "do not comment" look, but Frances had no intention of saying anything. They sat in Frances's' old car with the engine running and the heater on full blast to combat the chilly day.

Frances gazed out at the autumnal beauty of the scene before her and, after a short while, Jenny began to crumble in the presence of the kind stranger. She tearfully asked for a reason why her mother chose her father over her three children, leaving them to live with strangers. Frances could only offer a shoulder to cry on, acknowledge her heartbreak, and tell her she wasn't alone in having such unhappy memories. She told Jenny she didn't know if she'd ever be able to understand the consequences of her father's violence towards her mother.

Chapter 31

As she got a little older, Jenny sometimes visited her parents but never stayed overnight. She became accustomed to witnessing her mother's lack of vitality, confusion, and self-neglect. However, it was Kaye's stories about her nursing career that fascinated Jenny, leading her to want to be a nurse herself. On these occasions she saw enthusiasm sparkle in her mother's eyes. When she was eighteen, Jenny moved out of Mary and David's home to stay in her hospital's residential accommodation.

Jenny would never describe her childhood as happy. Certainly, there were times when life was bearable, even enjoyable, but those times were always tinged with sadness because they were not being shared with her mother. As they got older, the three children drifted apart and never recovered the closeness of their early years. Mary and David were always encouraging where Jenny's education was concerned. Mary was sometimes bewildered by Jenny's irritability but, all in all, her life in care had been a triumph according to her carers and social workers. Mary was truly mystified when Jenny broke off all contact from the moment she moved out.

Jenny was elated by the freedom of her new situation. Many constraints were lifted and, feeling invigorated, she set about her independent life with gusto. She was a shrewd manager and made her flat pretty and comfortable despite the meagre amount of money at her disposal. She was not so accomplished when it came to her choice of boyfriends; compliments and gifts, no matter how small, would leave her at their beck and call. The ending of these relationships was always difficult for Jenny. She would spend hours ringing old boyfriends and crying pitifully when her calls weren't answered or their telephones were switched off. She never let those who knew her witness any of these episodes and became skilled at hiding her feelings. She managed her emotional immaturity by focusing on her studies, and it wasn't surprising that she achieved top grades and assurances that she was destined to go far in her chosen profession.

The pregnancy resulted from a drunken romp with a married physiotherapist. The rather charming physiotherapist, James, turned out to be not so charming when told of the pregnancy, successfully requesting an immediate transfer to another hospital for "personal reasons."

Jenny was determined not to recreate the misery she and her brothers had suffered. Soon after Frieda's birth, Jenny found good child care and returned to work. She saved enough to put down a deposit on a small house and, when Frieda was one, they moved in. "It's a little palace for us both," she told her colleagues. With few social outlets, Jenny was isolated and bored. She started going out, visiting crowded bars where she enjoyed the anonymity and the warm glow of the alcohol. On some occasions she was able to arrange a baby sitter, a young local girl who had advertised in the local sweet shop. When the girl was unavailable, Jenny left Frieda alone, telling herself that the child never woke during the night and that she would pop back throughout the evening to check on her.

On the night of the accident, Jenny was not going out for the evening; she'd simply slipped out to buy cigarettes from her local shop. Because of the ensuing chaos it was a while before a neighbour alerted the police to the possibility that there could be a child in 22, Chelsea Road. The front door was forced and Frieda was found in bed, safe and well, but confused by all the disturbance around her. Meanwhile, Jenny was being rushed to the nearest Accident and Emergency Unit which happened to be where she worked. For her colleagues it was an upsetting time when Jenny was pronounced dead shortly after her arrival.

Chapter 32

"What's up, Jenny?" asked Andy, "you're very deep in thought." "Mmm."

"Hey, look at that. It's snowing in Manchester. Pretty picture, hey?"

"Maybe," said Jenny.

With such a leaden atmosphere it wasn't long before Andy retreated to his room. Mentoring this uncommunicative bitch would be difficult for the most experienced mentor but, for him, impossible. It was a formidable task given that he'd only been responsible for his own selfish existence prior to arriving at the Holding Station. It seemed to Andy that he'd been wrong in thinking that Barrie was fond of him or, if she did like him her feelings were certainly not straight forward. He guessed she was intent on making him more thoughtful and responsible by landing him with this difficult protégée.

Andy thought she'd made a mistake and that the job was beyond him. It was also inconvenient in terms of his relationship with Alicia; the demands on his time would reduce his opportunities for seeing her, and he would miss their contact dreadfully. Andy considered his options and found there were very few. He decided to get Jenny a transfer, realising he had to act quickly and decisively to prevent further damage to his reputation.

"But, Peggy, with all her nursing experience, surely she'd be better placed in Health," Andy wheedled.

"Can't be done, not until 26 successful *requests* have been completed and, as she's only just arrived, that's out of the question. There are other reasons, but they're not relevant here. Now, if there's nothing else, I'll get on," said Peggy.

Andy's contingency plan of coercing Alicia into mentoring Jenny had to be abandoned as he was concerned that Barrie was far more knowledgeable about his activities than he'd previously thought. His duty, made clear by Barrie's instruction to "guard her with all your might," was seemingly unavoidable - and filled him with despair.

Sarah seized her first opportunity to share her concerns with Peter regarding Andy's suitability as a mentor for Jenny. Even Sarah's composure was ruffled by Peter's response. He searched for Andy, intending to remind him of his responsibilities but couldn't find him.

He and Sarah both knew that Andy would be with Alicia, but neither of them said anything. They didn't know anybody else who flaunted the rules and regulations quite so openly, but a validation of their concerns would have consequences neither wanted to trigger.

Chapter 33

Sitting on her bed, whiling away the time, Jenny noticed the empty photograph frame - and gave a piercing scream. Sarah, on her way to offer the reassurance and support that wasn't forthcoming from Andy, heard the scream and rushed to Jenny's room. She was lying, face down on her bed, and refused to move. She was in shock having realised she was permanently separated from her precious daughter. Through her sobs and snuffles, Sarah could just make out that Jenny was repeating Frieda's name over and over. Jenny was too upset to grasp the comforting hand Sarah proffered. Sarah could not have quelled the torrents of tears, but neither did she want to. She sat in silence beside Jenny's bed, stroking her hand as she looked around, taking stock of Jenny's room. It was obvious to Sarah that there had been time to prepare for Jenny's arrival and, by taking personal responsibility, Barrie had ensured precision planning and a smooth entry.

Sarah was disappointed by Barrie's choice of mentor. She had reached an agreement with Barrie when accepting her own position, that she would be responsible for Jenny when the time came. Sarah regarded Barrie as an astute woman, and rarely found cause to criticise her, but leaving Jenny at Andy's mercy seemed irresponsible, especially as she had been separated from her child.

Jenny was inconsolable for a long time. Whenever Sarah thought Andy was being neglectful she would check, hoping to see some evidence that he was trying to help. This was seldom the case and Sarah was left clearing away untouched food before sitting beside Jenny, gently stroking her hands and face. She kept Andy informed about his protégée's progress, but he showed little interest in her or in Sarah's suggestions that she needed help.

When Jenny felt ready, she emerged from her room, rather dishevelled and her eyes red and swollen. She was angry, very angry, when Peter said her request to see Barrie would be refused. When he tried to reason with her by explaining that it was Andy's responsibility to assist her, she became even more infuriated and thumped on every door as she went along the corridor, shouting "that lout is neither use nor ornament!" In response to Jenny's need, Sarah took decisive action. When she knocked on Andy's door it came as a surprise; it wasn't often that his colleagues bothered him.

"Jenny was upset earlier and has gone back to her room yet again. Goodness knows I've tried to persuade her not to spend so much time alone, but she won't budge," Sarah told him.

"She'll be alright. Besides, I've got to respond to the *request* I'm dealing with, so would you mind doing the honours and dropping by her room?" Andy asked.

"I'll do my best, Andy, but you're the one who's responsible for her."

"Great," Andy thought; his delaying tactics had given him a slight reprieve - enough to allow him to spend some time with Alicia before having to return to his desk.

Chapter 34

Request.

Child requires emotional support. Swivelling his chair to face the screen, his back to his colleagues, Andy deliberately snubbed Sarah. It was irksome having to take responsibility for his actions and so, with a measure of consternation, he flicked the screen button to "On", and tuned in the picture. He could make out a smartly dressed woman in her sixties, clad entirely in black, her arms cradling a young girl, telling the child her mother was "living with angels." Unable to cope with the image, Andy joined Peter and Jeff for coffee.

"Have you seen Jenny today?" Peter asked him.

"No, Sarah's with her. I can't cope with her tantrums and, besides, I've been remarkably busy."

"I was under the impression that she's your responsibility," said Peter

"Really?"

"Irritating bastard," thought Andy. Waiting for a chance to arrange a reunion with Alicia, he wasn't bothered about dealing with his new ***request***. Instead, he took to tidying his desk, clipping papers together and filing them in the "Completed Task" cabinet. No doubt they'd be sorted out during the hustle and bustle of the pre-inspection weeks. Sarah and Peter looked on in disbelief as Andy fiddled about his desk. Jeff was too engrossed in the racing results to notice what was happening.

Jeff had successfully persuaded the IT Department to pipe the racing results onto his screen in exchange for his promise to sweet talk Peggy. He saw Peggy every day when he gave her the records of the previous day's activities. By using all the charm he could muster he dissuaded her from any spiteful actions she might be considering, such as delaying the return of their laundry, or shredding the new edition of the clothing catalogue from the Fashion Department. In this way he was able to keep abreast of his real passion, gambling. His favourite outlet was horse racing, but he'd consider anything so long as the odds were good enough.

Jeff was unaware of his unpopularity prior to his arrival at the Holding Station but, if he had been aware of it, he wouldn't have let it trouble him. While his leisure was devoted to gambling, his business was making money, and he'd been extremely successful. His wealth was his passport into the same enclosures as the rich and famous. The pinnacle of his success came about when he bought a racehorse called Thunder. He was ecstatic when, only a year later, the trainer advised running the horse in a race, assuring him that Thunder was "trying."

Jeff was never particularly interested in the company of women and his relationships, rarely lasting more than a few months, were ruthlessly terminated if he was questioned about his business or his gambling. His attitude to relationships led to him losing touch with his relatives after his parents' deaths. Because he made little effort to maintain contact with people, his own funeral was sparsely attended. He and Thunder had been electrocuted when parading round the winners' enclosure, and the irony of this was not wasted on the handful of mourners.

Andy seized his opportunity when a kerfuffle arose during the evening change-over. Proficiently, he located the torch and was outside in a flash, revelling in the peace and tranquillity. He savoured every moment of his excursion to the Fashion Department. He glanced towards the other buildings on the horizon, veiled in mist, and wondered what went on behind their tall walls and closed and shuttered windows and doors. He gave them little thought, however, preferring to dwell on the forthcoming warmth of Alicia's inviting body. Having become such a welcome visitor he no longer had to wait for someone to let him in. He walked freely along the brightly lit corridor into the main working area. When Harold, the sole occupant, told him that Alicia was engaged in discussions with Barrie, he thought he hid his disappointment quite successfully. Alicia and Barrie were trying to resolve the disquiet about the new uniforms, which John and Sandra were busily attempting to re-design.

Harold assured Andy that Alicia wouldn't be very long, and the pair of them settled into the comfort of two bucket chairs. They exchanged general chit-chat for some time before Andy found the courage to ask about Peggy. He'd wanted to broach the subject on other occasions but had been thwarted by the presence of others. Now he had his chance and, grasping the nettle, he made a start.

"I believe you were married to Peggy but, when you both arrived at the Holding Station, you asked to be placed separately," said Andy.

"That's right, lad. My goodness, the gossip gets around. We were married for forty years. I liked the woman, a fine wife and mother, but when I retired I found it difficult to live with her. I wasn't retired long before I ran the car into a tree, killing us both. I was sorry about that, took her away from the children and grandchildren, When we arrived here I just couldn't face the strain of being with her all the time, knowing that I'd caused such sadness by taking her away from everybody she loved. I do wonder if I was a bit hasty when I asked Barrie for separate postings. I must say there are times when I miss her. She doesn't look at me now, and she doesn't come to our events."

Their conversation came to an abrupt end with Alicia's entrance. She looked quite glorious, even in her rather ordinary uniform which she'd improved with the addition of some heavily carved, metal, jewellery. She was clearly tired, however, and Andy realised his hopes would not be realised. There had been complaints about the style and allocation of uniforms. Alicia didn't know the source of these complaints, but Andy felt certain that Jenny had something to do with them. "She's trouble that one, "Andy told Alicia," complained about the uniform on the first day. She's rarely been out of her room for days, but she has the sympathy of the rest of the team, though I don't know why." Alicia walked with Andy to the front entrance. Before parting, they shared a passionate kiss.

Creeping through the Earthly Team's lounge, Andy was relieved to find the room deserted and his indiscretion apparently undetected.

The following morning, at Sarah's suggestion, a tired and fragile Jenny reluctantly joined Andy, who barely noticed her, his attention being focused on the events unfolding on his screen. Jenny was bracing herself for the worst, fearing that her situation may have deteriorated beyond even her ability to put things right. However, her eye was drawn to Andy's screen and she was stunned to see her grandmother, Joyce, trying to console Frieda.

"How on earth did she get to be with that witch? I hate her! I bloody hate her!" Jenny shouted. Sarah rescued her and supported her limp body back into her own room where she cried without pause until sleep came to her rescue. Predictably, Andy stayed in his chair, idly watching his screen, trying to figure out why Jenny had been so upset. Mesmerised by the unfolding scene, he only realised the green light flashing on his desk when Peter's bellow brought it to his attention.

Barrie's summons was irritating. Surely she wasn't about to add to his already heavy burdens? He casually unwound his long body from his chair and wandered into Reception. Peggy was nowhere to be seen and he guessed she would be having a cigarette outside. Feeling more than a little roguish and nosey, he poked about in Peggy's affairs.

"I met Harold the other day," he said. Peggy puffed silently on her cigarette. "He seems like a decent man; spoke affectionately about you," Andy went on but, with no response from Peggy, he was forced to let the matter drop, and move swiftly on to his real reason for being there; Barrie's summons. Without a glance or a word, Peggy turned her back on him and went to her desk where she activated the technical process that would bring the escort. While this was being done, Andy skulked outside. He had mixed feelings when he saw Jim approaching. He was pleased to see him, but somewhat anxious because Jim's original friendliness had been replaced with something sterner when they last met. Andy was desperate to rekindle the warmth of their first encounter. The loss of Dave and Joe, the absence of real friends, bore heavily on him, and his team colleagues were no compensation. Presently, his main comfort was to be found in Alicia's arms, but she couldn't take the place of a mate. Andy thought his one chance of a decent friendship lay in his relationship with Jim.

Today he was not to be disappointed; Jim's demeanour was friendly and relaxed during their stroll to Barrie's office. He particularly asked how Jenny was settling in.

"It's difficult to adjust to this way of life, as we all know," said Jim.

"True enough," Andy replied, "but she doesn't seem to want help from anybody other than Sarah. I'm at my wits end trying to find a solution. If you have any suggestions I'd be grateful. It might get me out of a stressful situation."

"Befriend her, spend as much time together as you can, and she'll come round. You may come to value one another, "Jim said.

When Jim said goodbye, Andy was left feeling a little uneasy without knowing why. He hovered outside Barrie's office until he could delay no longer. It had been dreary outside and, in Barrie's warm and comfortable room he felt the chill of her brusque reception. She was terse and didn't offer Andy a coffee or a seat.

"I'll come straight to the point, Andy. I asked you to look after Jenny and that means *you* taking responsibility for all aspects of her wellbeing. Do you know what I mean by that?"

"Yes."

"We refer to this place as the Holding Station. On Earth you called it Purgatory. We feel our name is a little softer and appropriate as it suggests movement."

"Wow!" exclaimed Andy, "what are the choices?"

"They will come later. Explain to me," Barrie continued, "how you intend to meet the expectations placed upon you?"

"I have already shown her around the building and introduced her to the team and, of course, Peggy. I have explained the workings of the molten rock and how it activates the fax machine. I consider it prudent to explain our work in detail and have purposefully not given her any *requests* because I don't think she's capable dealing with them effectively as yet," said Andy. He hoped this would be sufficient to satisfy Barrie, because he had nothing else to offer, but Barrie hadn't finished.

"Do you realise that Jenny has been troubled for several days? I have been reliably informed that during this time you have not played a significant role in helping her to overcome her distress. Whilst I accept that you are willing to show her the fundamental workings of the job and plan to leave her without any **requests** for the time being, it is clear that you have personally neglected her. I expect you to rectify this situation immediately," said Barrie.

Andy shrivelled into the small boy being scolded by his father. The resurgence of old feelings rendered him as impotent as they'd done when he was a child. Andy was ill at ease with his own emotional imbalances, so helping with someone else's emotional needs was simply out of the question. The one exception was, of course, his mother, but she had always deflected his attempts to help so he had never experienced being able to provide comfort and resolve someone else's problems. Now his hand was being forced into "trouble shooting", difficult at the best of times, but especially hard when the person was as dislikeable as Jenny.

"More effort is required," Barrie went on, "I want you to return to your rooms, locate Jenny and find out, from her, what she needs. Surely even you could not have failed to see how upset she's been."

Yes, right. Yes, I will, if that's what you want," said Andy.

"It is. And I'm sure my instructions were made perfectly clear the last time we spoke. That's all I have to say on the matter."

With Barrie's back turned on him, Andy retreated rather swiftly, via the washroom, to splash cold water over his face, gather his thoughts and recover his self assuredness.

"Everything OK?" Jim asked him.

"Fine. Barrie needed to make sure I was clear about her instructions regarding jenny. We'd better get moving. There's something I need to do as soon as I can."

"That's me lad."

The pair engaged in some small talk, with Andy particularly keen to avoid any detailed discussion. With his trained eye he could see the direction the torch was taking, thereby allowing him to quicken the pace.

Chapter 35

Not for one moment did Andy intend to suggest that his meeting with Barrie had been anything other than a success, and he radiated self-confidence on his return. His preening was to no avail, however, as there was no one in the lounge apart from Jeff, and he showed no interest in him or his meeting. A disgruntled Jeff told him that Sarah and Jenny were ensconced in Jenny's room having obtained special permission from Barrie to meet in their private accommodation.

Andy thought Jeff was jealous, after all, he was accustomed to constant attention from Sarah which he dismissed or accepted on a whim; now her attention had switched to Jenny. Needing to make an immediate start on Barrie's instructions, Andy knocked on Jenny's door. There was a short delay before the door was opened - by Jeremy! Jeremy's presence was such a surprise that Andy's composure evaporated, leaving him stuttering. "Not now, old boy, maybe tomorrow," said Jeremy. Andy felt he was in limbo. He didn't relish returning to Jeff's company, which would be even less pleasant if Peter decided to join them, and he couldn't do anything about Jenny just yet. His confusion and unhappiness turned his thoughts back to the comfort and relief that Alicia could provide, but this was not an advisable option in the circumstances.

It was still early and, with time dragging, he decided to take a look at the *request* from the previous day. To his surprise the monitor was switched on. This was strange as he was always careful to switch it off to stop anyone prying into whatever he was doing. The house on the screen was modern with small rooms (unlike Andy's childhood home) that were furnished and decorated to make the most of the limited space. In each brightly painted room hung several framed, contemporary, posters of pop stars and actors. On the wooden floors, chosen for easy maintenance sat a couple of IKEA sofas. Bookshelves lined several walls, their shelves bowed under the weight of the books they carried; children's and adult's literature alongside text books on nursing. The house was modern and bright, very different from the more conventional one he'd viewed the previous day, although the child and adult were the same. The pair, Andy correctly surmised, were in the child's bedroom. Both crying as they looked at the photograph in the little girl's hand, although neither was touching the other.

Andy was inclined to turn off the monitor, being unable to fathom what was expected of him. Being an isolated child he'd had difficulty in forming friendships. His only friend was Gordon but, as Gordon was a popular lad, their time together had been limited. With little experience of social conversation he was embarrassed when engaging informally with adults. His most rewarding relationships came about when he was forced to leave home and find a flat. His father had ruthlessly evicted him after he'd failed his final examination and become unemployed. Right now a "fix" with Dave and Joe would lift his mood and give him some respite from his difficulties. The monitor was closing down and he was about to lift himself out of his chair, when the woman said "I miss Jenny too." Quickly he rebooted the monitor and had another look, he saw the child's belongings being packed into a sports bag.

"Frieda, we have to go to my house," said Joyce.

"I'm going to stay here. This is mine and mummy's house and I'm not going with you. I hate you and my mummy said you never loved her," said Frieda. "Bloody hell," breathed Andy, "Jenny died leaving a young child."

When questioned by Jeff about Sarah's whereabouts, his nonchalant shrug made certain he would scurry away as Jenny arrived flanked by Sarah and Jeremy. "What do they think I'm going to do to her? he wondered, whilst projecting a broad grin towards the emerging party.

"Glad to see you, old chap, "Jeremy began," Sarah and I have some joint work we need to complete today. Jenny, we'll leave you in Andy's capable hands."

There was no escape for Andy. He had to comply with Barrie's directions; he'd lost whatever status he'd had, and he knew it. He would have to forget any notion of continuing his relationship with Alicia, in the short term at least. Jenny refused his offer to get the coffee but found the gesture pleasing and the act of kindness, albeit late in the day, was welcome and refreshing.

Encouraged by her mentor, Jenny sat beside him watching as events unfolded before her. She was having to grapple with the knowledge that her precious daughter was lost to her and living with her great grandparents, and that she could do nothing about it. Jenny took her mother's view of them as being uncaring and selfish, as demonstrated by their reluctance to offer her grandchildren a home and leaving their fate in the hands of strangers.

"Come on, I'm sure it will help if you see what's happening," Andy said. Being chivvied along in this way, by Andy of all people, irritated Jenny. Her response: "How would a spoilt bastard like you know what's good for me?" was equally offensive to Andy. He wanted to shout back at her and then walk away and leave her to her own devices, but his predicament made it advisable to compromise. "Jenny, I have to understand why you're so angry with your grandmother."

"Because," said Jenny, "she's a devious little bitch who was only ever interested in her work at the bank and very expensive hair and nail salons. Oh, and buying Nicole Farhi clothes."

"Whose clothes?" asked Andy.

"Not important."

"Surely it would be wise for her to care for Frieda?"

"D'you think? Well let me tell you something. That woman let me and my two brothers live with foster carers before she would look after us....cow! For all our sakes, she should have died before me and my mother. Anyway, why isn't Frieda with my mum?" Jenny fell silent as she realised her daughter was not with her mother because Kaye had stayed with her alcohol soaked husband. Consequently Jenny had to rely on her hardnosed bitch of a grandmother and her husband.

Holding his arm loosely around her shoulders, Andy encouraged Jenny to look at the monitor. Once tuned in the screen showed a clear picture of Frieda in the park feeding ducks, their feast provided by

Jenny's grandparents, Joyce and Sam. Frieda looked petite and pretty in her tailored blue coat, her blond hair cascading down her back. Frieda was absorbed in her task and unaware of her great grandparents' distress as they cried on each other's shoulders. Jenny listened intently as the couple mulled over the past trying to be reasonable about the unreasonable. Joyce's love of fine clothes was indisputable. She was also proud of her home, her husband, and her daughters' accomplishments.

Her older daughter, Justine, had a successful career as a financial adviser. Having courted the terribly reliable John for a couple of years, the couple married. The families lived some distance apart but didn't allow this to spoil anything. Every effort was made to organise delightfully exciting times with the couple and their two children.

Kaye was more strong-willed than her sister and certainly not keen to take advice. School posed few challenges for her academically or socially and she sailed her way to academic success. A notable feature was the sense of style she inherited from Joyce. Sam and Joyce were surprised when their somewhat self-seeking daughter chose to pursue a career in nursing. By the age of twenty-one, armed with a degree, she was working on the Accident and Emergency Unit of her local hospital. The hospital environment with its daily hustle and bustle excited Kaye and she determined to have fun and marry a handsome doctor. Nothing was further from her mind than falling in love with a plasterer working in the hospital. When Sam and Joyce met Ronnie they understood why Kaye found him attractive. He was handsome, smart, athletic, and delightfully gracious. At Christmas and on birthdays he gave generous gifts. When dining out he took pride in dealing with the bill. Any stumbling or loudness on Ronnie's part was put down to tiredness following strenuous work. After a couple of years, Sam and Joyce were delighted to give their consent to Ronnie and Kaye's marriage, and they were impressed that the couple were in a position to buy their own home.

The wedding was a lavish affair, befitting the couple's expectations; Joyce and Sam were only too pleased to make a significant financial contribution. Sam's sensible investments had resulted in them being financially secure. Kaye looked charming in a long, white crepe dress which clung to her slender figure. She was holding cream lilies and a floral display mingled beautifully with her long blond hair. Justine complemented her sister by choosing a scarlet dress which flattered her nearly black hair and brown eyes; the fresh flowers entwined in her hair made the perfect finishing touch.

Sam swelled with pride as he walked his daughter down the aisle of their local church. He and Joyce had no misgivings over their daughter's marriage. It was a cold, autumn, day but the sun was shining brightly as both families assembled for photographs that were full of happiness and optimism for the future. The reception was an equally extravagant affair with good food and drink and excellent entertainment. Joyce and Sam had met Ronnie's parents on a couple of occasions before the wedding. Ronnie's father, Graham, was also a plasterer, and his mother, June, worked in the local Marks and Spencer store. Towards the end of the evening, as guests were beginning to leave, Ronnie became embroiled in an argument with his best man, which was rapidly defused by Graham. The happy couple left for their honeymoon with very little attention being paid to the altercation; it was simply attributed to "wedding nerves."

The couple returned bronzed and happy, and were even happier when they moved into their own home. In the early days Kaye and Ronnie often visited their parents but, by the end of their first year together, Joyce noted a slight decline in her daughter's moods. Sam saw nothing particularly noteworthy and blamed his daughter's lack of sparkle on her pregnancy.

Jenny was born ten months after the wedding and baptised soon afterwards. The service was followed by a barbecue in her parents' garden. Everyone enjoyed the free-flowing alcohol and the lively music piped through speakers on either side of the patio. Throughout the day and early evening, Kaye was clearly feeling tense. When she suggested the party should move indoors to avoid disturbing her neighbours, Ronnie became loudly angry with her. For the first time, Sam saw the cracks in his daughter's relationship that his wife had been aware of for some time. He was more than a little ruffled by the sight of his charming daughter humouring her husband. As they drove home, Joyce said, "I told you something was wrong. Haven't you noticed how seldom she visits nowadays? She's always making excuses, and she never has new clothes. All her money is spent on Jenny and Ronnie, it's a disgrace!"

"I think you might be exaggerating," Sam replied, "Of course, I didn't like what I saw today, but I think Ronnie probably gets a bit tense in large gatherings and drinks too much. It'll pass over, you'll see."

"What's more," Joyce went on, "did you notice his mother never stopped watching him? I swear she knows something isn't right, and I wonder how long she's known that he has problems....probably fuelled by alcohol."

The remainder of their journey passed in silence as they reflected on the scene they'd just witnessed, although neither of them envisaged the drama that would unfold over the coming years.

Sam and Joyce gradually saw less and less of Kaye. Their other daughter, Justine, tried to visit, but Kaye always discouraged her with a barrage of excuses. Not even the births of two more children, Craig and Sean, made any difference. Kaye kept her distance which prevented relationships developing between her family and her children. There were occasional exceptions when, out of desperation, Kaye was forced to approach her parents. One of these occasions came shortly before Sean's birth.

"We're going to lose the house unless you can lend us the money. I've been to the bank but they absolutely refused a loan as Ronnie doesn't have a permanent job. It's a real bind - I just don't know where to turn. Can you help?"

"But Kaye, dear, you already owe us several thousand pounds which we loaned you after Jenny was born," said Joyce.

"We just can't continue to bail you out," her father said.

"Just one more time, please Dad; the building trade isn't doing well just now and Ronnie hasn't had any work for the past few months."

"That's strange," Sam said, "I thought the building trade was doing well and plasterers were in great demand."

"Maybe, but Ronnie isn't, and I've no idea why," Jenny said.

"We'll see what we can do, but this has to be your last loan. Your mum and I aren't wealthy and we've had quite a lot of expense over the past few years, what with you and Justine getting married."

Clutching the cheque, Kaye left as soon as was reasonable as she needed to get home to placate Ronnie and avoid another storm. Kaye loathed begging for money and seeing the pity in her parents' eyes but, most of all, she missed them.

"Well, they're loaded aren't they?" Ronnie said, "and it'll make them feel virtuous- well your mother anyway. She can brag to her mates, it's what she likes."

Kaye knew her husband's criticism was far from the truth. She doubted whether her mother ever talked about her or the children, thinking she was probably too embarrassed. Kaye's joy following Jenny's birth was less evident after Craig was born, and even less when Sean arrived. Joyce and Sam managed to be part of the family's life until Ronnie's drunkenness spiralled out of control and the bruising on Kaye's slight body increased. Time and again, Joyce and Sam pleaded with Kaye to leave her husband, with the guarantee of a new beginning for the children and herself, but she never accepted their proposals. Withdrawing was desperately difficult for Joyce and Sam and their decision was made with genuine regret and sadness both for themselves and for the depths to which their family had sunk. They very rarely saw Craig and Sean again, and none of their loans were ever repaid.

Chapter 36

Jonathan introduced himself to Joyce as the Clarke family's social worker and updated her and Sam on their daughter's situation. Kaye and Ronnie had moved to rented accommodation when their home was repossessed. The reason for his visit was to discuss the children's future and the possibility of them living with Joyce and Sam; "the law requires this." The court process was over, having concluded that the children would not be returned to Kaye and Ronnie. Now it was necessary to make plans for the children's long term futures. This would entail moving away from their placement with Auntie Joan, which had been a temporary arrangement.

"That's where you come in," Jonathan said, "Of course, we could offer a great deal of support, including some financial remuneration."

Sam and Joyce spent the next couple of days doing nothing except considering and discussing Jonathan's proposal, sometimes including Justine in their deliberations. During this time they had little sleep and barely enough time to eat. Since retiring, they'd moved into a small, compact, bungalow in a picturesque village. They had established a new, and amenable, life style and had many friends with whom they shared similar interests. Of course, they could move back into a larger house with sufficient additional accommodation for three children, a house closer to the children's schools, but they feared becoming trapped, again, in a situation where they had few options of their own and would be obliged to witness their daughter's suffering each time she saw her children. With heavy hearts they decided to reject Jonathan's proposal. Most of this was unknown to Jenny having been forgotten, distorted over time, or misrepresented by her father.

Several years later Joyce received a telephone call from another social worker. She heard about the accident and Jenny's death." I understand," the social worker said," that you saw your granddaughter periodically while she was placed with the Thompsons, and that you knew about Frieda." Joyce readily agreed to take charge of Frieda. It eased the uncertainty she'd lived with since she and Sam had made the decision not to do the same for Jenny and her brothers.

Collecting Frieda from the hospital, where she'd been examined and declared fit, was a sombre experience for Sam and Joyce, especially when they saw their world weary daughter heading for the mortuary, presumably on her way to identify Jenny's body.

Chapter 37

Andy was finding the situation too difficult, so it was a relief when Sarah joined them.

"Can I get you two a coffee, "Sarah offered," or something to eat? You've been hard at it for hours, and probably need a break."

"Yes, that would be great," Andy said. He was startled when his telephone rang as it was a rare occurrence these days.

It was Alicia, her voice piercing, in stark contrast to her usual, melodic, tones. She was annoyed because Andy hadn't been in touch. She accused him of not being "focused on their relationship" when he knew full well that she was under pressure concerning the new uniforms. Despite Alicia's unusually abrasive manner there was little Andy could say or do to calm her. Barrie's instructions meant it would be foolish to promise to visit, and with Jenny and Sarah nearby he could do little more than offer a brief apology before returning the phone to its cradle. He knew his apology and the promise to visit "when possible" would not go down well with Alicia. Meanwhile, Jenny had chosen to take her coffee outside and have a cigarette, which Peggy provided after some expert negotiating by Sarah,

Chapter 38

Mary was reading the final chapter of her book, and keen to finish it, when her peace was shattered by the delegation crossing through her office on its way to the Board Room. The group was headed by the sports complex Managing Director, George Sinclair. Mary was his personal assistant. Mary took pleasure in her elevated position although she had achieved it on merit. She had an impressive array of qualifications and credentials. The first hour of her first day had presented Mary with her first dilemma. George had insisted that she should call him by his first name. He was amused when she switched back and forth between the informal "George" and the formal "Mr. Sinclair." Mary had found that respect for the more traditional structures during her education, as well as in business, was generally appreciated, and she found it difficult to change. Over the next few years, George watched Mary mature into a gracious woman who handled staff with courtesy and skill; she made his job much easier, and he was genuinely appreciative.

Mary had never considered the matter of George's retirement and was shocked when he announced that it would be in three months time. "They've got time to recruit properly," George told her, "I'll make sure they find someone decent. I can't have you thrown to the wolves, can I?"

Of course, the interview and selection processes took time but, finally their prime candidate, David Thompson, was given the job. Today was David's induction and several managers were hustling him, intent on lobbying for their own departments. "This is Mary, my personal assistant," said George, "She's excellent and will be an asset, particularly while you're learning the ropes." "Nice dress," David said.

Mary and David worked together for quite some time before they became romantically involved. It was amazing how quickly their romance developed once it started. Having agreed to marry David, Mary also agreed that it would be best if she found another job as working together could compromise either or both of them. In no time, Mary found another, better paid, position that was also nearer to home.

The couple's first child, Percy, was born eighteen months after their marriage. Mary was delighted with motherhood, leading David to suggest that they should become foster parents as "this would give us the opportunity to share our good fortune and happiness." When their second son, Gareth, was born they decided against having more children of their own, but to continue to foster "vulnerable young children." David recommended that they should focus on younger children so their influence would be greater and last longer. Mary was pleased to agree with him. She was also grateful for his willingness to become involved. He was always prepared to drive some of the youngsters to and fro while Mary took care of the others and kept a well-ordered household.

Chapter 39

Fiercely attempting to dig the frozen earth did little to ease Mary's anger, and she all but ignored the pain from the throbbing blisters forming on her hands. She didn't even notice the three stones lying under the sycamore tree but, if she had, she still wouldn't have had any idea about their part in her life.

Her tortured thoughts were constantly drawn to the events of a few nights ago when the Police arrested David, and took him into custody for questioning. The next day the Police had interviewed her, as a witness. At a moment's notice Mary's father, Granddad Johnson, had stepped into the breach to look after his grandsons while Mary was with the Police officers. The questioning followed several avenues, the main one relating to the games David played with their foster children. It was many years since Jenny had told Mary she no longer wanted to play David's game of hide and seek. Mary thought this was strange as Jenny appeared to enjoy the game when all the children were playing it, a point also made by David. Jenny hadn't mentioned the matter again because the games ceased.

Jenny was summoned to Reception to meet Detective Rebecca McGreevy. They found a quiet room and the detective asked Jenny to describe living with Mary and David and what, if anything, happened when she was alone with David. The questioning took Jenny back to a time she hadn't thought of for quite a while. She knew the detective was alluding to the game of hide and seek, which David had said "would be their secret." Jenny described how David would tickle her as he dropped sweets down the front of her school blouse before slowly retrieving them. After this, if there was enough time - and as an extra treat - she dropped sweets down the front of his trousers and gently retrieved them. If she was too quick, the game had to start all over again. David described it as their "secret, special game," but this never impressed Jenny. When David wouldn't stop playing the "game", Jenny told Mary and the "game" was never played again.

It was another child who alerted the Police. She had lived with David and Mary before Jenny arrived and had mistakenly construed David's behaviour as a form of love and affection. It was the birth of her first child that prompted her to go to the Police, and they had launched an extensive enquiry involving all the children fostered by the Thompsons.

The scale of the consequences of a missed opportunity staggered Detective McGreevy during an interview with referees who'd supported the Thompsons' application to foster. David and Jasmine Jones had had time to reflect on their decision not to mention David's agitated and controlling behaviour towards Mary during a mini-break in Cornwall. They'd attributed it to the strain and stress of a new baby. "Perhaps, had we been more honest, the painful experiences for several children could have been avoided," Mr. Jones admitted.

Charged with sexual assault, David's bail conditions stipulated that he must reside at a designated bail hostel. Before being shown to his room, he read and signed the notice of his bail conditions as well as the rules of the establishment itself. It was all quite unnecessary as a couple of hours later, he was found hanged in his room.

"The bastard!" Mary's ranting didn't ease the chaos in her mind. Now she had to decide how to impart the devastating news to her children. The charges against David had been reported in the evening newspaper, but at least they'd been spared the distress of a trial. The children were still at school and Mary had to decide between remaining in the town or moving away into the anonymity she craved. Moving would spare her boys the inevitable unpleasantness of stares and whispers, gibes and taunting, but it would be expensive and she no longer had David's salary and the fostering had been suspended while investigations were ongoing. Mary finally decided to close up the house, move the boys to different schools, and move in with her father who, as it turned out, was a wonderful support.

Chapter 40

Stunned by Harold's presence in Reception, it took Peggy several moments to collect her thoughts.

"Yes, what can I do for you? A bit off the beaten track aren't you?" she said.

"Well, you forced this upon yourself by not responding to my messages, "Harold replied.

"What do you want?"

"I need to arrange a transfer."

Without a moment's hesitation, Peggy walked right past him and out of the rear door, lighting a cigarette as she went. Harold was forced to follow her. He'd always hated her smoking and it appeared to him that she was deliberately blowing clouds of smoke in his direction.

"Can't face it anymore," he said.

"And what might that be?" Peggy asked.

Harold tried to explain the reason for his request, but the smirk on Peggy's face was disconcerting. He told her the Fashion Department had deteriorated since Andy's arrival. "He's not a bad lad. Maybe a bit nervy and edgy at times." Harold went on to say that Andy's relationship with Alicia had caused tensions and the more embroiled Alicia became, the less work was completed. The general atmosphere had also worsened with the arrival of the new woman, Jenny. "Then there's the complaint," Harold said," I'm not totally sure who made it, but the perceived wisdom is that it was Jenny. The problem is the women-only ruling. It never bothered Sarah; she belongs to an older generation and, as a nun, she was used to wearing a uniform. But Jenny's a different kettle of fish. The complaint was a particularly bitter blow for Alicia. She's spent months in consultation to come up with the new design, and she was chuffed with the end result, which Jenny was the first to model. The fall-out when Barrie told her she had to withdraw the design was unmerciful. So... that's it in a nutshell," Harold finished.

"Ammunition at last!" thought Peggy. She finished her cigarette and stubbed it out firmly, a deliberate show of strength and control. She promised to search the "vacancies" and advised Harold to return in a couple of days. Harold did return, and then had to repeat the process over and over again, always leaving disappointed as his hopes were dashed on each occasion.

Peggy became absorbed in all the varied possibilities at her disposal. Her search of the Medical Department was the most exciting as she remembered Alistair was still working there. Indulging her meanest instincts, she visualised Harold cooped up alongside Alistair in the confined space of the Sterilisation Unit, where his patience would be sorely tested. Although she was still very angry with Harold, this transfer would be too cruel for a man who had travelled widely and needed freedom of movement.

Eventually, Peggy negotiated a transfer to Journalism, but only on condition that he let Alicia know that he had requested the transfer. Harold was not best pleased with the condition, believing it would lead to conflict - and he was right. Alicia was furious, accusing him of being irresponsible for leaving during such uncertain times. Peggy's insistence brought home to Harold how he'd always gone to any lengths to avoid confrontation, usually choosing the sanctuary of absence during his many seafaring years. He now appreciated that his request to move to the Fashion Department had reflected badly on Peggy whom he'd subjected to a painful and humiliating experience.

Some eight weeks after making his request, Harold's transfer was completed and he moved to the offices of the Nirvana Chronicle. Peggy called Tracy, the hairdresser, and arranged for a complete cosmetic overhaul before choosing herself some elegant new clothes. Only Sandra and John were at the exit to bid Harold farewell; Alicia excused herself, claiming she had a deadline to meet.

Chapter 41

The Nirvana Chronicle building was some distance from the Fashion Department, so Jim and Harold decided to fly. This delighted Jim who loved his lively old aeroplane. The torch was still required as Jim's navigational skills had not improved, so Harold held it out of the window and Jim followed the rays, only occasionally correcting his course when going off beam. The journey took longer than anticipated but they didn't mind as they were having so much fun, recklessly twisting and turning while sharing a pipe filled to the brim with tobacco. As Harold disembarked, Jim raised the issue of Andy. He'd been reluctant to do this earlier because they'd been having so much fun "department spotting" through the clouds. Disrupting their game would have been stupid as fun was something of a scarcity.

"Quite a troubled young man," said Harold.

"Mmmm."

"I had little to do with him, but he often seemed agitated and didn't want to spend time with anyone but Alicia," Harold said.

Just a few days later, having found what he needed, Harold used the screen to contact Peggy and ask for another meeting with Jim. He was surprised to find Peggy looking much more attractive and he thought there may have been a hint of friendliness in her voice. Still, Peggy took some convincing about the need to book Jim, saying he was a bit expensive. She relented, however, when Harold told her that privacy was essential. Closing the screen, Harold was pleased with his success and even wondered if he'd seen a twinkle in Peggy's eyes.

"Found it when making myself familiar with the archives," Harold told Jim.

"NEWS INTERNATIONAL

Three men were found guilty of the murder of Andy Goodyear and received life sentences for their crime. In his summing up, Judge Jones acknowledged that Mr. Goodyear had taken a significant amount of heroin, but said his death was caused by the brutal and sustained attack perpetrated by the defendants."

The girl with Andy on the night he died, told the Police that the attack started when they were leaving a nightclub. The gang separated the couple and the onslaught began. In her statement she said the argument followed an accusation about the "impurity of the heroin."

This account went some way to explaining why Andy had so often been anxious and irritable, especially when he'd first arrived. Jim guessed that Andy's initial incapacity and confusion had been a blessing for Barrie and the Influencing Team as it gave them time to discuss the implications of Andy being accepted onto the Holding Station. Of particular concern was his personality which could be expected to disrupt any department in which he was placed. Barrie had told Jim of the Influencing Team members' distaste for the proposal to admit Andy. She considered Andy had been dealt an unfair hand when alive and with the stability of the Earthly Team he could redress the consequential imbalances, so she had used all her persuasive powers procure this opportunity for him.

Harold added a few more pieces of hitherto unknown information dealing with events after the attack on Andy. He had not died immediately, but had spent many days in Intensive Care before his parents decided to switch off his life support apparatus. In truth, it was Stuart's decision and he'd coaxed Vanessa into agreeing with it.

Andy's funeral was sparsely attended and solemn. Dave and Joe were there alongside Andy's parents and grandparents. Dave and Joe only found out about the arrangements via a chance meeting with Vanessa a few days beforehand. Jean and Frederick left immediately after the funeral service, overwrought with grief which they realised could turn to anger directed at Stuart that could compromise their daughter's safety.

Chapter 42

Request.

"Replacement bow-tie needed."

"Your first ***request***, Jenny," Andy said. As soon as she read its contents, Jenny knew that Andy had deliberately chosen this particular ***request*** for its relevance to fashion, she felt sure he'd done so out of spite and in retaliation for her complaint about the new uniforms which had so angered his girlfriend. Replacement clothing had been slow to come over from the Fashion Department, but this didn't bother her as Peggy had sent an array of clothes for her to choose from and, in fact, seemed delighted to help her.

"Why should I help that privileged tosser?" Jenny complained. "He shouldn't have been off his head on his stag night and forgotten to pack one."

"Come on, Jenny, it's all part of the pre-wedding festivities," coaxed Andy. Jenny was outraged to discover that the cosseted barrister, Philip, hadn't managed to get himself adequately attired in time for his nuptials in a few hours time. Jenny could barely bring herself to deal with the matter but, having no choice, she prepared her desk and tuned in the screen. She noticed one of the two men, whom she took to be the bridegroom, frantically ringing his guests in the same hotel asking to borrow a spare bow tie. The scene was being watched by the other man, presumably the best man, who was clearly amused. Having no luck, Philip made his desperate plea for help which prompted the molten rocks to rumble, activating the fax machine.

Jenny couldn't think of an alternative to contacting the Fashion Department. She crossed her fingers and hoped Sandra or John would answer the telephone, but she was out of luck. Once Alicia recognised

Jenny's voice her genteel manner became very frosty, although she allowed Jenny to arrange a bow tie be made available via the hotel receptionist. The marriage actually took place without the groom wearing a bow tie. Philip said he couldn't exchange such solemn vows wearing a yellow tie with red polka dots. Reception staff told him it was the only bow tie they could find, but he was sure it was "somebody's idea of a joke."

"Right. That's done," said Jenny. She was about to file the *request* when Andy caught sight of it.

"Why on earth did you do that?" he asked.

"Felt he deserved it. You know, the same as Jane did," Jenny replied.

"Jane? Don't know what you're talking about."

"Jane. You never sorted out her wedding dress, simply arranged for Graham to work in Saudi."

"I don't think she did too badly."

"Really?"

"Who told you about Jane and Graham?"

"Sarah, when she completed part of my induction in your absence. You were probably with Alicia. By the way, she didn't sound too happy when I spoke to her; she wants you to give her a call."

Chapter 43

It was that time again, and Jim was taking Andy to see Barrie for his latest review. Tentatively, Jim broached the subject of Andy's death and the surrounding circumstances, but the response was not what he'd hoped for. Andy's mind was on other things and he showed little interest in what Jim was saying. Andy was preoccupied with thoughts of seeing Alicia, but being harnessed to Jenny - "The Angel Without Mercy" - was making it impossible.

"Did you deal in heroin?" Jim asked him.

"Er.... occasionally, " Andy said. Stunned by Jim's question, he was relieved, for once, to arrive at Barrie's office. He was also glad that their meeting was pretty straightforward and free of the usual fractiousness, because he'd been thrown off balance by Jim's earlier question. He wondered if the others had any inkling about his Earthly Life, and the possibility hit him hard. A large part of his previous existence had been submerged by recent events, but now it was surfacing again. And what, Andy asked himself, was the significance of Jeff's "not allowed to say" when he was questioned about the previous tenant of Andy's room? Was his anxiety warranted? For the present, his only crumb of comfort was Barrie's comment that he was "making reasonable progress."

On his way back to the Earthly Station, Andy was amazed to find himself thinking in terms of "going home". He'd never felt at home anywhere and now the strange notion was associated with a cold, corrugated, building!

"Surely you must see that I had to deal, "Andy said to Jim, "I had no other choice. I couldn't live off the benefits and my father refused to give me any money. The only help I had was when Mum popped down with some food."

"No other choices?" queried Jim, "What about Sheila?"

"Who?"

"Sheila, the woman whose electricity was disconnected. You thought she should manage on her benefits."

"Oh."

They finished their journey in silence. Andy fumed over Jim's challenge, being tied down by Jenny, and being unable to visit Alicia.

"Have you signed in?" The booming voice came from Reception. Peggy had been replaced by Rex, a bumptious, forty-something, army sergeant who had died, prematurely, killed by a ricocheting bullet at the end of the Second World War. Rex was not persuaded by Peggy's insistence that it would be impossible to master every aspect of his new job without help. "Not so!" he barked, and took up the position immediately.

"Hello, Andy," met the new chap yet," asked Sarah. She whispered that clandestine negotiations had been taking place for a few weeks. During these meetings sensitive issues between Peggy and Harold had been smoothed over, and certain disagreeable matters had been resolved. The upshot was that the pair had become reconciled. Jim had been pleased to escort Peggy to a rendezvous with Harold shortly before he'd taken Andy to see Barrie. He'd put soft lighting in his plane and left the windows open to reduce the stale smell of tobacco. The couple's reunion was touching, even romantic, and it brought a tear to Jim's eye.

Chapter 44

Rex taking over in Reception was likely to increase Andy's difficulties while, quite unfairly according to Andy, his protégée was taking up even more of his time. He was suspicious of the strengthening bond between Sarah and Jenny who spent hours huddled together in front of screens. He couldn't see that it derived from mutual respect and the comfort to be had from a supportive relationship. Sarah cajoled Jenny into appreciating the reason why Sam and Joyce chose to throw their daughter a life-line after Jenny had died. Many years had passed since the children had been taken from Kaye and Sam and Joyce had burdened themselves with the decision not to have their grandchildren living with them. They felt the time had come to seek out their daughter and offer her their support again.

The trio closed their ears to Ronnie's snoring as they passed through the dingy conditions of the living room into the kitchen. Kaye was a sorry sight, feeble and crushed by her life but, with her parents' encouragement, she followed them upstairs and collected a few items of clothing before leaving the house. Happy and relieved, they ignored Ronnie's final rant. Once inside the sanctuary of her parents' home, Kaye's pain began to ease. Joyce filled the bath and poured fragrant oils onto the running water. Sam cooked lunch. Childhood memories of such care and love flooded back to Kaye, but they were much tarnished by other memories of her recent life. Frieda stayed with Auntie Justine while Sam and Joyce helped Kaye to find a flat and to convince a range of professionals that she had left her marriage behind her and that Frieda would be safe living with her. From the springboard of awfulness came some of the happiest times for Kaye, but there was always an undercurrent of sadness.

During these heartening moments, Sarah confided to Jenny that

she had listened intently to her *requests* for snow, and had been saddened by her inability to act. Given that she had never appealed for
help with David, Sarah had been unaware of her predicament.

"There was an enormous hullabaloo when it all came out and
David committed suicide. The best we could do was to delay your
arrival and bring Andy's forward, "Sarah said." David, "she went on,"
wasn't a particularly easy bloke to get along with, he was always complaining that he'd been dealt an unfair hand. He was especially keen
to deal with *requests* that involved anything that seemed unfair or
illegal. His lack of impartiality meant that Peter had to exert a tight
control over our Morning Meetings. Whenever disagreements arose,
David became outraged and demanded that Barrie should arbitrate;
on almost every occasion she agreed with our majority. When it was
clear that you would eventually be coming, it was a dreadful task
getting him to leave. He protested against the decision that he should
go, claiming it would be 'great to catch up with' you. He even insisted
that he hadn't 'done much.' Days dragged by as each attempt to move
him came to nothing. Eventually he was forced out by having his food
machine switched off. He went off in a blazing temper and we haven't
seen him since. Jeremy managed to paint over his name and replace it
with Andy's. We tried to discover his whereabouts, but Peggy said the
information was confidential and wouldn't budge."

Chapter 45

With Rex officiously monitoring all movements in and around the Holding Station, making arrangements to see Alicia was out of the question for Andy. She'd become more and more difficult to manage of late, constantly telephoning and demanding to see him, then becoming angry when Andy couldn't oblige. Jenny's complaint had been upheld and the new uniforms had been discontinued. Alicia felt that Harold had abandoned her, and now there were rumours that John wanted a transfer as well. With fewer staff and declining production, the Fashion Department was in disarray, which was making her miserable.

Chapter 46

With blood gushing around her brain, Alicia died instantly. At just thirty she lost her life to a brain haemorrhage and ended up lying in a fast flowing stream guarded by her dog. When she failed to arrive home at the usual time her husband, Thomas, contacted all their friends but eventually conceded defeat and rang the police. Initially, of course, they suspected him of having a hand in her disappearance, and were a little disappointed when she was found along with her trusted dog.

According to Alicia she had been happily married to Thomas for six years and they had been planning a family before her untimely death. Naturally, as she told everyone who would listen, there were times when the couple had their differences, but they were soon resolved. In fact, Alicia had manipulated Thomas, who was besotted with her and demonstrated his love by showering her with magnificent gifts well beyond his ability to afford.

Thomas told his family and friends how he had only insured his wife a couple of months earlier, and had not understood what had prompted him to do it. Fortunately, however, devastated though he was, he was able to repay his debts with the sizeable insurance pay-out.

Thomas buried his beloved wife in the village churchyard. Her parents and many of the couples' young friends were in attendance. When the last mourner left their home, Thomas packed a bag, locked up the house, and handed the keys over to an estate agent with instructions to sell it along with all its contents. He never did return.

Over the years, he married a couple of times and fathered several children, but he never stayed around very long, leaving each relationship with minimal notice and fuss. He was never able to rediscover the love and camaraderie he had with Alicia. Thomas's predicament led his uncle, Jeremy, to question his decision to advise Barrie to admit Alicia to the Holding Station.

Andy's attraction for Alicia was purely sexual. She found him irresistible and she never hesitated to break all the rules in order to be with him. She thrived on the intensity of her feelings but they could become unmanageable which sometimes led to indiscretion, a lack of caution, and a tendency to allow herself to become vulnerable. Andy, she had to concede, gave her sexual highs that she never enjoyed with Thomas, pleasure that permeated every part of her physical being. She'd never felt as much a part of any other man as she did with Andy.

This man - or lout - was playing havoc with her emotions and belittling her. When they were together she was sure of his love and affection, but her confidence disappeared when she was unable to see him.

The problems began when Jenny came on the scene. She not only prevented Alicia and Andy getting together, but she had also caused the unpleasantness in the Fashion Department with her complaint. In fact, she'd caused chaos in the short time she'd been on the Holding Station, She would have to go.

"You can't just walk in," Rex challenged Alicia, but before he could intercept her, Alicia strode into the Earthly Team room, frustrated by not finding Andy at his desk, darted into the lounge where she found Jeremy reading his newspaper. Jeremy was horrified by Alicia's unwelcome appearance and had no idea how to handle the situation. He was sure she wasn't aware that he was her husband's uncle, or that he'd had a hand in rescuing Thomas by bringing Alicia to the Holding Station. He'd been on the fringes of Alicia's company many times, where he'd found it relatively easy to avoid direct contact with her. Now he was being forced to tackle her growing anger head on. He was greatly relieved when Andy and Jenny emerged. The furore gave Andy no option but to coax Rex into relaxing his application of the rules, allowing him to escort Alicia back to the Fashion Department, reassuring him that he had the means to get there and would soon return.

He tried desperately to persuade Alicia that his love for her was unchanged, attributing his lack of attentiveness to the pressures brought to bear by Barrie's instructions. Despite all his verbal and physical protestations, Alicia was not convinced. She thought his interest was shifting to Jenny, but she said nothing.

The second troublesome event of Jeremy's shift occurred when the red light on his desk began to flash. Nervously he located the torch, signed the Destination Book, and headed off in the direction of the Influencing Teams Department. He assumed, correctly, that his summons was somehow connected to the disharmony between Andy and Alicia. During his journey he reflected on his dishonesty to Andy when he'd told him the Influencing Team had given him the option to move from, or remain with, the Earthly Team. The truth was that he'd signed away his freedom forever to procure an agreement that he could bring Alicia to the Holding Station. Now Head Office presumably wanted him to explain why he'd failed to forestall the catastrophe that would result from Andy transferring his affections to Jenny; an event which was threatening the stability of the Earthly Team. Jeremy had agreed to report all matters of concern within the Earthly Team in exchange for being allowed to arrange Alicia's arrival on the Holding Station. Jeremy's discussion with the Influencing Team's Director, Matthew, focused on Alicia and David.

Alicia was proving difficult to manage and David was still being kept in the outer wilderness pending decisions being made about his future.

Jeremy and the Director concocted a plan and agreed that it would only be divulged to Barrie.

Chapter 47

Jeremy knew it was just a matter of time before the ***request*** came through. He was grateful that it arrived during his shift, avoiding the morning discussion as to who would deal with it.

Request

Please can I have my wife back in my arms? It was the opportunity that Jeremy had been waiting for, and it had arrived more quickly than expected.

Alicia was eager to accept Jeremy's offer to arrange a meeting with Andy and delighted by his promise to make himself scarce. In a flash, Alicia changed into a striking and stylish outfit. She declined Jeremy's offer of coffee and food, not wanting to delay her meeting with Andy. Sometime later The Nirvana Chronicle reported the events which ensued, describing the incident as a most unfortunate and unavoidable accident The article didn't cover the whole story that whilst retrieving a ***request*** from the fax machine Alicia slipped into the molten rock and was sucked back to Earth. Although Alicia was now known as Alice and looked nothing like Thomas's dead wife, he was sure that he had his wife back and was ecstatically happy. Alice was not certain she wanted to marry Thomas, but she was unable to extricate herself, so they married, moved into a new house, and even bought a dog. Jeremy never again involved himself in relationship problems, no matter whose they were.

The green light flashed on Peter's desk and, true to form, he immediately gathered up his papers and headed for Barrie's office where she and Matthew were waiting for him.

"Are you sure the team don't know why you're taking the lead?" asked Matthew.

"I feel they're irritated by the position I've taken, but they haven't challenged me. What should I tell them about David's whereabouts?"

"The truth," said Barrie,

"But I'm not sure what it is," Peter said.

Barrie explained that Jim had taken David to Pluto on his way back to resume his life on Venus.

"Of course," Barrie said, "David's struggling to keep warm on Pluto, and has some difficult work to do there. Once he's finished he should be ready to start his rehabilitation programme; all told, it should take several millennia. In the meantime, most of the current team members will have moved on."

At the next team meeting, Peter gave an account of David's circumstances and drew everyone's attention to the article about Alicia in the Chronicle. He wasn't sure if there was the trace of a grin on Andy's face.

Over time, Andy and Jenny came to understand, and accept, that although they'd had very different childhoods, they'd suffered similar experiences. They both knew the fear and dread of violence where there should be love. Neither could claim to be in a better or a worse situation than the other and so, grudgingly, they came to accept each other's position - but never without a protracted dispute beforehand.

About the Author

McQueen

Social work was not choice more destiny. Initially I was employed as a residential worker caring for young people who had been placed in secure accommodation. The reasons for their incarceration would never be considered today.

My interest whetted I decided to develop my knowledge and experience by moving into the specialist area of child protection and mental health. This work, over several decades, gave insight into the complexities of family life and the impact on children's development emanating from domestic violence and substance misuse. The most staggering revelation was parents' desires to avoid intervention by professionals but without the knowledge and skills to do so.

It is clear that domestic violence, drug misuse and sexual abuse is not confined to a certain income group, it is the ability and choices available to manage their complexities.

I appreciate all I was taught by the families and individuals I was privileged to work with as well as my own children, Andrea and Gillian.
Thanks to Brenda Wilson and Gill Cooper for their input and especially, Jim Scragg for his time and effort.